THE
· WALNUT TREE ·

ALSO BY CHARLES TODD

THE
WALNUT TREE

Charles Todd

WILLIAM MORROW
An Imprint of HarperCollinsPublishers

HarperCollins books may be purchased for educational, business, or sales promotional use. For information please write: Special Markets Department, HarperCollins Publishers, 10 East 53rd Street, New York, NY 10022.

FIRST EDITION

Designed by Joy O'Meara

Library of Congress Cataloging-in-Publication Data

Todd, Charles.
    The walnut tree / Charles Todd. — 1st ed.
        p. cm.
    ISBN 978-0-06-223699-9
    1. Young women—Fiction. 2. Nobility—England—Fiction.
3. Nurses—England—Fiction. 4. World War, 1914–1918—
France—Fiction. 5. World War, 1914–1918—England—Fiction.
I. Title.
    PS3570.O37W36 2012
    813'.54—dc23

                                                                2012031037

12 13 14 15 16   OV/RRD   10 9 8 7 6 5 4 3 2 1

Mystery bookshops——old bookshops——independent bookshops are disappearing at a rapid rate, and this is a sad loss for everyone who loves books. A handful of book people are bravely daring the odds by opening new ones. We met just such a bookshop in Anaheim, California, specializing in mystery, fantasy, and sci-fi—— complete with café and fireplace. We wish them all the best.

Now comes the sad news that an old and dear friend is shutting its doors.

So to you, Partners & Crime, we dedicate this latest Charles Todd. We wish you were going to be there to celebrate it with us. We just wish you were going to be there. Period.

We owe you guys. More than we can repay. And we love you all.

Thanks for the memories.

And as Maggie put it, "God, we had a blast." Just knowing you all.

• *Chapter One* •

I was in Paris the day the French Army was mobilized.

And so began the Great War for the French. But not yet for the British . . .

When I left England, on an overly warm July morning in 1914, war clouds were gathering, but most of us believed that little more than posturing would come of it. And then war was upon us, and there was no time to think of anything else.

I'd traveled to France to visit Madeleine Villard. She'd been a classmate at L'Académie des Jeunes Filles in Paris, where I'd been sent to learn to speak French without a Scots accent. And I was in the wedding party when she married Henri. Now she was heavily pregnant with her first child, due in September, and was ordered not to travel to the Villard country house up in the cooler Marne Valley.

She begged me to come to her in Paris, and I did, promising to amuse her and keep up her spirits.

Henri, her husband, was not as optimistic about the chances of war, but he put on a good face in front of his wife, to spare her any worry. Her brother, the handsome Alain, called nearly every day, and at first I thought it was concern for his sister that drew him to the house so often. I learned soon enough that it was my presence that brought him. I didn't quite know how to respond. Whether to be pleased or amused.

The truth was, I'd had such a schoolgirl crush on Alain. I hadn't told anyone, not even Madeleine.

At the end of each term, he had come to Paris to fetch Madeleine home, and every girl in the school stood with her nose pressed to the window glass to see him arrive. Tall, fair, already come down from university, he set hearts aflutter. I had met him again at Madeleine's wedding, but he had still seen me as the schoolgirl acquaintance of his sister, and in the midst of the wedding festivities, I doubt we'd spent more than five minutes in each other's company, save at the dinners and parties that were part of the celebration. He had danced with me once, an obligatory dance, but Madeleine had been over the moon with joy.

"I can't think of anyone I'd rather have as my sister," she'd exclaimed as he brought me back to where I was sitting and, duty done, gone off to more exciting partners. I'd glimpsed the lovely brunette on his arm earlier in the evening.

I didn't have the heart to tell Madeleine that his interest was perfunctory and very likely to stay that way. I'd outgrown my infatuation, of course, but I still found Alain immensely attractive and exciting. Sadly he didn't appear to feel the same way about me, and I'd tried to be philosophical about that. Much good it did me.

Now I was no longer a callow schoolgirl. I'd made my debut into society and had achieved the sophistication that came with the rigorous training for a presentation at Court. I'd also come into my inheritance from my mother, when I was eighteen. She had died when I was only three years old, leaving my father and me to cling to each other in our grief. I think that was why he seldom let me out of his sight, for fear of losing me as well. Neither of us ever got over her death. It would have pleased my mother that I'd grown up as independent as she had been, free to choose my own clothing, much to the despair of my second cousin who was now head of the family. He had no daughters, only sons, and it was his opinion that young ladies should dress demurely. White muslin, blue satin sashes, the sweet and innocent fashion that was so popular. My father would have understood my liking for something more elegant, but then my father was dead. Cousin Kenneth had not only inherited his lands and his title, he'd also inherited me in the form of guardianship.

"That rose gown you wore at the ball last evening," he'd said to me not six months earlier. "I should have thought something in pale blue or lemon yellow might be more suitable."

"I'm a black Scot," I said. He and his family had flaming red hair. "My dark hair is unsuited to pale colors. I look as if I'm dying of consumption."

He grinned. "Surely it isn't that bad."

I couldn't help but smile as well, but I stood my ground all the same. "You aren't a woman, Cousin Kenneth. Ask Cousin Catriona. She'll understand." His wife was known for her excellent taste in all matters of dress.

He said in exasperation, "How am I to find a husband for you, my dear? If you make it so difficult? You're as headstrong as your father was."

"I'd rather choose my own husband, if you please," I told him. But I knew how unlikely that was. By the terms of my father's will, I was Cousin Kenneth's ward until I was thirty. My father had wanted to protect me, in the event he wasn't there. And to my great sorrow, he wasn't. Had he known— had he had a premonition that he would die young?

The suggestion made my cousin frown, and there was an undercurrent of worry in his voice as he asked, "There isn't anyone you have particularly in mind? Someone you met in London. Or France? Someone . . . unsuitable?"

To his credit Kenneth had been very forbearing. But he also took his duty seriously, and in the end, he would insist when he felt it was in my best interests.

"I'm not likely to run off with Gypsies or one of the ghillies," I answered as lightly as I could. When that didn't erase the frown, I said, "No. You needn't worry that I'll do anything so foolish. I know what I owe to my name and my station. Still, I'd like some say in the matter. After all, I'm the one who must live with your choice." My parents had married for love. It had also been a very fine match. I was discovering how rare a thing this was, in my circle.

"I've had several very fine offers for your hand, Elspeth, and I can't go on putting them off. You must understand that your husband is your future, and it's not a matter to treat lightly." And then he'd added, "If there's a war, the eligible men will be the first to die."

I could only promise to remember his good advice.

And now here I was, in France, Alain Montigny suddenly realizing that I exist. The more I saw of him, the more I liked him. I could easily imagine spending the rest of my life with him. He reminded me a little of Bruce, Cousin Kenneth's middle son. Perhaps that's why I felt so comfortable in Alain's company.

Madeleine was always finding new ways of throwing us together. Concerts. The opera. Dinner parties. Whatever invitations she could persuade Henri to accept on my behalf—after making certain that Alain would also be present. Poor Henri became, unwittingly, the matchmaker.

"She cannot stay cooped up in my rooms all day. And you know how I fall asleep in the evenings. She's used to London society," she had told her husband. "We must contrive amusements for her. After all, look how happy she has made me. I want her to be happy too." She'd given me an account of the conversation a few weeks later.

Henri, bless him, was a lovely man who cared deeply for his wife and spoiled her without reservations. But we talked on these excursions, he and I, about the war, and one night as we were returning from a dinner party, he said to me, "England isn't involved at the moment. That could change. You speak French like a native, but your papers are British.

If the Germans can't be stopped, you could find yourself accused of spying."

I hadn't considered my own danger. Still, I said, "Surely there's plenty of time. As long as Germany respects the frontiers of Belgium, England won't come into the war."

"Yes, well, I think our own frontiers with Germany are too strongly fortified. She will have to come through Belgium even if it forces England into the war."

I'd heard one of our acquaintances in the War Office mention the same possibility before I left London. It was not very comforting to find that Henri believed it would happen. Not now with Madeleine's baby on the way and my friendship with Alain daily growing into something more. Was it love I felt? Surely it must be. We had such wonderful times together. There were outings in his motorcar, picnics in the countryside, evenings sitting side by side at the theater or a dinner party. Henri or one of Madeleine's friends chaperoned. I lost count of the number of people who told me what a handsome couple we were, he so fair and I so dark. Even strangers, like the priest in Chartres or the woman in the flower shop outside the gates of Versailles. The French are far more forward than the English in matters of the heart.

Alain said one afternoon as he brought me back from an excursion to St. Denis in the motorcar, "Would you find it so very hard to live in France, Lady Elspeth? It's a very long way from Scotland."

But my heart was no longer in Scotland. Not since my father's sudden, tragic death. We had been close, he and I, and I mourned him still. It was his love of speed—in boats, motorcars, even an aircraft—that had made him the most exciting man I knew. And it was his love of speed that had killed him. Lord Douglas had lived as his ancestors had, with that Highland spirit that had led them to follow Bonnie Prince Charlie and die at Culloden Moor rather than bow down to the King of England. There's a portrait in the gallery of the castle showing the Prince and one of my ancestors and another man standing together in the courtyard of the castle as it was then. And my ancestor could have been my father, down to the elegant way he stood in his kilt. Like a prince himself.

I had always known my own mind, and so had my father.

I said, "I have no close ties to Scotland these days. I've lived in England for the past two years." In a house in Cornwall that had once belonged to my mother's brother, a lovely old stone mansion that overlooked the sea and was said to have been built by one of Drake's captains in the days of the great Queen Elizabeth, she of the Armada and a love for handsome, dashing men.

"And you finished your schooling in France."

I smiled. "So I did."

"I remember you from those days. The prettiest girl in the room by far, and with a dignity that was impressive in one so young."

I hadn't thought he'd noticed me. And he most certainly had no time for me at his sister's wedding.

As if he'd heard the thought, he said, "At the wedding

you were still too young. And I was still too green to think of marriage. I had the world to see and conquer."

"Then it's fortunate that I came back to Paris."

"Not fortunate. It was my suggestion to my sister." He grinned. "And she didn't require a great deal of urging."

A conspiracy. I didn't know whether to be amused or angry. I wasn't used to having my life arranged by others.

As we were turning into the courtyard of the Villard house, he glanced in my direction and saw my expression.

"I have already made plans to go to England in September, as soon as Madeleine has her child. Perhaps you'll allow me to escort you home. I'd like very much to meet your cousin."

"Ah." It was all I could manage to say, for one of the footmen had come up to hand me down from the motorcar. But my thoughts were flying in every direction. If Alain asked my cousin Kenneth for my hand in marriage—he had all but told me he would—what would I say? What answer would I give? Suddenly I had no idea.

"Would you mind?" Alain asked as we walked into the cool foyer of the Villard house. His gaze was on my face, but I didn't look up.

"I should think you and Cousin Kenneth enjoy each other's company." And that, I told myself, was as silly a response as I could have come up with if I'd had weeks to prepare my answer.

A gentleman never spoke of marriage to a lady before addressing the head of her family. But Alain had asked my permission, in a roundabout way, and I could have said no, in the same polite fashion. It was a kindness on his part to consider my feelings, and as I was to learn, Alain was always thoughtful.

"It's agreed then."

And with a smile as he touched the brim of his hat, Alain went to his house to change. I stood looking after his motorcar and found myself wondering what better answer I'd have given, if I'd had a little time to think through his question.

What would Cousin Kenneth think of a Frenchman? I smiled to myself. A little lower than a Gypsy, because he was foreign? My cousin wasn't overly fond of foreigners. He had said so often enough. But then it wouldn't be Kenneth who married one, would it? And while there was no title in Alain's family, his blood was probably bluer than mine, his fortune larger. A suitable match in every sense.

But was I in love with Alain?

How could I not be?

I turned, running up the stairs to tell Madeleine about our drive—but not about our conversation.

And then the Germans marched. Without considering anyone else's plans but their own.

What's more, they marched not across the well-defended German-French border, but through the tiny, fairly new country of Belgium. The Belgians were fighting gallantly from all reports, but it appeared that they would be over-whelmed in a matter of days. Refugees poured into France, bringing tales of hardships, wholesale looting, and atrocities with them.

The British issued an ultimatum—withdraw from Belgium or face the consequences.

War, staring all of us in the face.

Madeleine was in hysterics when she learned that Henri had been called up, that his orders required him to report to his command immediately. No last dinner together, no lingering farewells. The doctor had to be sent for.

He feared for her child and told her in no uncertain terms that she must calm down or risk losing it.

I had to take her hands in mine and say forcibly, "You cannot send Henri off to fight the Germans, knowing this child is stillborn and that he must leave you to grieve alone. It would be too cruel, Madeleine. You must show him how brave you are, as brave as he is. Besides, there are rumors that the war will be over by Christmas. He'll be home by then, you'll see."

"But why can't they let him stay? Just until the baby is born? Why is that too much to ask?"

"I'm here with you," I said. "They must think one Highland Scot is enough protection for one baby."

She smiled against her will.

But it was the turning point.

An hour later, Henri was gone. Madeleine fell into a restless sleep, and I went down alone to eat my dinner. I met Alain, just coming through the door. He too was wearing his uniform, and my heart turned over. Not Alain as well? Not so soon.

"How is she?" He stood at the foot of the stairs, looking up.

"Better. But if she sees you like this . . ." I gestured to his uniform, my voice failing me.

"I know. But there's so little time. You'll have to be strong for her, Lady Elspeth." And then he turned, giving me his full attention, as if he'd made a decision. "Will you come out with me in the motorcar? I know how late it is, and how improper. But I must be gone before morning."

I didn't hesitate. "Let me fetch my shawl."

"I'll go to say good-bye to Madeleine."

And he was off, taking the stairs two at a time, bounding into his sister's room, his cheerful voice echoing down to me as he teased her lightly.

I went the other direction when I reached the passage and collected my shawl. I was in a turmoil of emotions. And I think Alain was as well.

He came down the stairs a few minutes later, his face grim. "I had to lie to her," he said quietly, leading me out to the motorcar and helping me in. "I told her I would be training recruits. You mustn't tell her any differently." He turned the crank, then got in beside me. "I think you've missed your dinner too?"

And without waiting for an answer, he drove out the gates and down the street to the turning he was after. It led into a maze of tree-shaded streets with well-kept and comfortable houses on either side. Ahead I saw the brightly lit windows of a small restaurant, and Alain pulled up beneath a sign that read LE CHAT BLEU. The Blue Cat. "This will do," he said and found a nearby alley where we could leave the motorcar.

As we walked back, he said, "This is a respectable restaurant. It serves meals to the middle class and sometimes to working-class people looking for a pleasant evening out. You will not be insulted by the clientele. I would choose somewhere better known, but I don't think we should be seen dining together. Not without a chaperone. And we won't be recognized here, I promise you."

We stepped through the door into a long narrow space with an ornate wooden bar along one side and small tables down the other. The walls were decorated with lovely posters—I recognized one from the Paris Exhibition, and another of a pair of smiling young women cycling together down a country lane, advertising bicycles. A third expounded the glories of Venice, a gondolier in front of the famous square gesturing toward it with his straw boater. They were the only bit of color in a very sedate atmosphere.

A few older diners occupied tables at the back. I wondered if their sons or grandsons had also been called up, for they seemed to have little to say to one another, their gaze on the middle distance, as if their minds were following their loved ones to whatever rendezvous point had been set out in his orders. So different from the Paris of only a few days ago, full of gaiety and laughter, untouched by fear. I looked up at Alain, tall and handsome in his own uniform—but he wasn't marching in a parade, he was going off to war. I suddenly felt like crying.

He led me to a table by the Venice poster, and then went to speak to Madame at the counter. Soon she was bringing out roast chicken, a dish of vegetables, and a basket of potatoes baked in the oven. Thick slices of bread came with a slab of butter, and a bottle of white wine. A plate of cheeses followed. Country fare. Simple but well prepared.

In spite of everything I had an appetite. The food tasted as lovely as it smelled. Alain was hungry too, and we ate in silence for a bit. Then he said, "It won't be long before the Germans have finished the Belgians. They'll be on our frontier in a matter of days. I think we can hold them. And your country has already massed its regiments at the Channel ports, if they haven't already crossed and marched toward Mons. They had agreed for decades to stand surety for Belgium's independence. They won't hesitate."

Men like my cousin Kenneth's eldest son, Rory. He'd be in the thick of it, a career officer and a good one.

Alain added, "I want you to go home now. While you can."

"But what about Madeleine? She was in such distress tonight, when Henri left. And now you. Alain, I *promised* her. She'll need me now more than ever. Don't ask me to abandon her to strangers."

He grimaced. I could guess how difficult their parting had been. "My sister will be all right. It's your safety I fear for. We have cousins, and Henri has a large family as well. She has only to send for them. They'll take care of her."

"But the baby—it's likely to be rather small, the doctor said—" I began, but he cut me short.

"God forbid that anything happens to it. But we must face reality. If Henri survives, there will be other children. The fact is, we have every expectation of stopping the

Germans at the Belgian frontier. But they will be aiming for Paris, you see. If we contain them, force them back into Belgium, all well and good, the war will be over by Christmas. If we fail, well, then, who knows?"

"That's a rather grim picture you've just painted. Are you deliberately trying to frighten me into going?"

"War is not for women. You have no idea of the hardships that lie ahead, even if we win. There will be shortages of food, of petrol, of everything. There will be few parties or concerts. Refugees will fill the city, to the point that nothing is the way it was. My sister is French, her child French. They must take their chances or move farther south, but you must go home. Elspeth, I care too much to let you stay in France, even for the sake of my sister. The fighting won't touch England, you see. Here, we and the Belgians will bear the brunt of it. I've been so grateful for all you've done for Madeleine. God knows I am, but I want you safely away."

It was an impassioned plea, and I thought I knew what must lie behind it. I was proved right when he put down his wineglass and said, "I want to marry you, Elspeth. I have no title to match yours, but is that so bad a thing? I am wealthy, I can support you as my wife, and I will take pride in seeing that you want for nothing. More to the point, I love you with all my heart. I have not spoken to your cousin—there is no way to reach him before tomorrow morning. But as soon as I am free of my military obligation, I will go to him. And here is a token of that promise."

He reached into his pocket and brought out a small velvet box. Flicking it open, he passed it across the table to me.

"It was my mother's ring. She wore it with pride as my father's wife. I offer it to you."

I took the box containing the ring and held it between my hands. Deeply touched, I could only stare at it. And think, looking at it, that he was marching into danger tomorrow. He would be facing an advancing army soon enough, an army already tested in its march through Belgium. What if he was killed in that early action? What if he came home lame or blind or without a limb?

I realized in that instant that what frightened me more was a single question. *What would my life be like without Alain in it?*

And like so many young women across France at that very moment, I took the ring out of its velvet box and handed it to him to slip over my finger. The dark red ruby with its circlet of diamonds flashed in the light of the candle on our table, and for a moment I could think only of blood. And then it was in place, warming my hand as he looked at me, his blue eyes just as warm.

"I have no right to kiss you," he said softly. "But just once—I would like it very much."

And in that quiet little café we rose to our feet, the table between us, and he kissed me on the lips, my hands in his. I think he meant for it to be a chaste kiss, but there was passion behind it, deep and swelling, as if to last a lifetime. And then he stepped back, smiled at me, and we sat down again.

I don't remember what we said in the half hour we lingered there. His voice was deep, his words reaching far inside me, and I wanted to remember them forever. But I couldn't. All I could think of was that tomorrow morning he was going to war, and I knew then why Madeleine had gone into strong hysterics. When you cannot change something, when you want so desperately to hold on to it, and you know it is as far beyond your power as the stars, something breaks inside.

In that moment I loved Alain too, and his ring, settling on my finger as if it had always belonged there, sealed that love.

I told you, didn't I, that I had always had a mind of my own.

Sometimes it's a blessing. And sometimes a curse.

· *Chapter Two* ·

PARIS WAS NEARLY EMPTY OF men the next morning.
Only the very old, the very young, the lame, and the halt
walked the streets, and they were a somber lot.

I hadn't told Madeleine about my evening spent in the
little café. I hadn't needed to. She touched the ring on my
finger, then looked at me with bright, loving eyes.

"You'll be my sister. Oh, Elspeth, you've made me so
happy I could almost forget that Henri has gone away."

I hadn't taken the ring off. It was like a talisman, a
promise that Alain would come back to me.

"It's a token only," I said. "There's nothing official. After
all, he hasn't spoken to Cousin Kenneth. We must have his
consent."

"Even your cousin Kenneth is bound to like Alain. But,
yes, it's not something to make public until he's done the
right thing. But between us, I'm so very very pleased."

She hugged me, then lay back against her pillows. "I wish
I could have gone to Villard to have this baby. If it's a son, he

should be born there. If the weather breaks, will you help me persuade the doctor that I should go north by easy stages? I'll even take a midwife with me, whatever he wishes."

I remembered what Alain had said, that the Germans would push toward Paris, that Paris was what they wanted. And if that was true, what better way to reach the capital than to come down the Marne Valley? Straight through Villard. I'd looked at a map last night, unable to sleep, walking the floor, and then descended to the library to discover what lay ahead of us. It didn't seem so terrible on the heavy map paper. Flat blue lines marking rivers, red dots marking towns. No concept of distance, or time. No way to judge what an army could do, marching through, cutting a swath of death and destruction. But I could see for myself that the Marne Valley was no place for a pregnant woman close to bearing her first child.

I said, "The weather hasn't broken. If we ask now, the doctor is bound to refuse. Let's be patient."

"But it's important to me. Henri was born there, his father and grandfather before him, and as far as I know, generations beyond that. It's a very old name. Famous, in fact. I think Henri would like to know that his child carried on that tradition."

She had got it into her head now, a surprise for Henri when he came home. I'd been warned by the middle-aged woman Henri had hired to oversee the nursery that pregnant women sometimes developed strange fancies. "My last lying-in," Nurse Berthe told me, "it was lemons. In season or out, Madame must have lemons."

This was a far more dangerous fancy.

"I know how much it matters," I said soothingly, plumping Madeleine's pillows. "But if the war is over very quickly, then Henri will be here to take you to Villard himself."

That satisfied her for a few days, but she returned to the subject several times over the following week.

And Belgium fell to the Germans. The British had declared war on Germany on the fourth of August, had sent troops. But the German Army was now poised to invade France.

The news was not good. The frontier didn't hold. Another week passed, and another, with rumors flying. The British Expeditionary Force was guarding the coast roads and finding itself overrun. Forced to retreat time and again. The French Fifth Army wasn't engaging the enemy. Refugees were clogging the roads, preventing the Allied armies from moving north. Disaster piled on disaster. Then the first refugees reached the city, bringing such tales of horror and suffering that her maid, Marie, and I tried to keep them from Madeleine. Villages, houses, even churches had been shelled, looted, civilians injured and killed, livestock and stores taken to feed an army.

We had heard nothing from Henri or Alain since their departure. Not surprising in the circumstances. But it would have been such a relief to know they were well.

The newspapers tried to keep up with what was happening, but events were outpacing their efforts.

On the day that we heard the Fifth and Sixth armies

were not able to stop the enemy's advance, that the Marne Valley lay open to them, Madeleine went into labor.

I could only thank God that we were not in Villard.

I had stayed on in France, despite the warnings from Alain and from Henri. But I felt I owed it to Madeleine. Now as I went out to find a taxi to summon the doctor, I saw a sight that I shall never forget for the rest of my life.

I had had to walk for blocks, no taxis to be found in any direction, and then just ahead of me, I saw them. All the taxis were gathering in a great cluster, as if drawn together by a magnet, filling the heart of the city, and soldiers were everywhere. The little Renaults were being stuffed with troops, and as soon as their doors were shut, they set off at speed for the north.

A man stopped next to me to stare at the spectacle and after a moment said, half in prayer, half in anguish, "It's a last effort to save the city. My God, have we come to this?"

I saw a French officer watching the scene, and I crossed to where he was standing, catching at his sleeve to pull his attention away from the taxis. "What's happening? What does this mean?"

He looked down at me, saw the ring on my finger, knew that someone I cared for must be in the army.

"We are losing on all sides. The Germans are advancing down the Marne. We are sending troops to stop them, and sadly, this is the only way. The trains—they will have to march too far, you see, if they use the trains. And there isn't time."

I stood there, mesmerized, as some six hundred taxis

took on their complement of men and then dashed toward the outskirts of the city. Would they be in time? Or was Paris about to fall? Someone in the northern suburbs was said to have heard the guns last night. The Villard porter had brought that news just this morning.

Tearing myself away from the unbelievable scene, I walked on to the house of Monsieur le Médicin. I found it in turmoil, packing cases everywhere, the furnishings hastily covered in dust sheets.

He was preparing to send his family south to Lyon, to safety, in the event the Army couldn't stop the German advance.

I reminded him that his patient needed him, and reluctantly he agreed to come with me to the Villard house, cursing as he went because there were no taxis, and his driver had already been called up, as had the Villards'.

We reached the house to find Madeleine in strong labor, and it was only an hour later that the child was born.

"A boy," the doctor came out to tell me. "A healthy boy. Nurse Berthe is here to attend to it and to the mother. Just now, I have a duty to my own family."

"If worse comes to worst—can she be moved?"

"Not for several days. There is the danger of bleeding and also the danger of infection. Keep everything around her and the child as clean as may be. That's her only chance. To put her into a motorcar just now—I couldn't guarantee anything."

I went up to see Madeleine soon afterward. She was fretting that there was no way to send word to Henri that he had had a son. "And I never got to Villard," she cried. "I had so wanted to have our child there."

"Paris is in danger," I told her flatly. "And the Marne Valley is a battlefield. Be grateful you aren't there."

She shuddered. "Truly?"

"Truly."

"What are we to do, then?"

"You must go south, to your family's house on the Loire. You should be safe enough there."

"But Henri won't know where to find me!"

"Of course he will. He knows better than we do that Paris isn't safe. He'll expect you to go away as soon as you can travel."

She smiled then, satisfied. But I wondered if Henri was still alive. Or Alain. There had been dreadful casualties, according to all reports.

I waited another few days, and by then, the news was better. The taxi army had arrived in the nick of time, and the Germans had been turned back.

I rushed to Madeleine to tell her the news, and her face glowed with relief and happiness. I hated to tell her what I'd decided over breakfast. But it had to be done.

"Madeleine. I came here to be with you while you were so uncomfortable with your pregnancy. And now the child is here and you're doing remarkably well—"

"You can't leave me! And there's Alain—he'll want to know you're here, and safe."

"Britain is at war, Madeleine. I feel as strongly about my country as you do about yours. I must go home."

"But what can you do there? It isn't as if you were a man and could enlist. Will you grow vegetables on the lawns of Cousin Kenneth's castle? Will you drive an omnibus in London?"

She was right. What could I do? But I was suddenly homesick, had been for several days, dreaming of my home in Cornwall, dreaming too about Scotland, which I hadn't done in years. Even the knowledge that it would take twice as long for Alain's letters to reach me in Cornwall couldn't persuade me to stay in Paris. I could come back to France, I told myself. Once I'd been to England.

"If our circumstances were reversed, would you stay on in London while France was being attacked?" I asked her finally.

"No, but then I have a husband here, a child. You have Alain."

"I'll come back, Madeleine. As soon as possible. But first I must go to England. It's—my cousins are probably already in the Army, friends I've danced with, that I've played tennis with, that I've dined with. They're in harm's way. I must go home and do something. Even if it's only to write letters, to keep up their spirits."

"And what about Alain? France is going to be your *home*. Stay here and wait for Alain to come back."

"I'm not his wife. Not yet. Madeleine, I must do this. And I think Alain would want me to go. He tried to convince me to leave the last time I saw him. And I need to finish my life in England before I marry him. Perhaps he understood that better than I did."

She gave me a sad smile. "If that's what Alain wanted, then of course you must go. But I wish you would stay."

"I wish I could." It was a white lie, for her sake. I touched the ring on my finger. "I kept my promise to you, didn't I? And I'll keep mine to him." I tried to smile, but it faltered. "He must ask Cousin Kenneth for my hand. Properly. Alain will come to England if he has to, to find me. Wait and see."

I tried to persuade her to go to the Loire, but now that Paris was saved, Madeleine wouldn't hear of it.

It was a sad parting, a few days later. Carrying only a single valise with the few things I would need on the journey, I left on the train for Calais.

Of course there was no one to see me off. The chauffeur had left to join his own regiment, and the driver of the taxi saw me only as far as the Gare du Nord, and no one had gone ahead to buy my ticket. I walked through the crowded railway station and dealt with arrangements. But as I was entering my carriage, the man who had been just behind me in the queue at the ticket kiosk said, "Allow me." He took my valise from me, settled me into my seat, and then found a place for the valise in the crowded compartment behind mine.

I expected him to take the seat next to me, but as I thanked him, he nodded, then went back into the corridor to find where he belonged. The passenger who did sit next to me was taciturn, and I was grateful not to have to make conversation.

The train stopped at every siding while troop trains

thundered past. And the returning trains, laden with wounded, headed south to the hastily erected military hospitals for those who couldn't be patched up in the field. Through the dusty windows I could see bloody bandages pressed against the glass, and I wondered how many of these men had raced north in the Paris taxis. If Alain or Henri or any of the men I'd met at the opera, a concert, even a dinner party, was aboard those trains. I tried to shut the thought out of my mind, focusing on finding the first available ship to Dover.

It was a strange feeling, to be torn between two countries.

It was not long before I could hear the big guns, thundering salvos that made the ground shake and soon had my head aching.

And then Calais lay just ahead. The French port was filled with British soldiers, coming, going, waiting.

There was a brief delay on our arrival, passengers asked to remain in their seats while an ambulance was brought to carry off a man taken ill during the journey. Stretcher bearers soon arrived; I could see them from my window. As they removed the passenger, the sheet covering him slipped a little. I recognized the kind man who had helped me with my valise. Even I could see that he had died.

I must have gasped or something, because the man next to me said curtly in English, "Heart. Must have been."

I turned, wondering if perhaps he was a doctor. But he was dressed more like a shopkeeper. I'd seen a number of expatriate Englishmen at the *gare* in Paris hurrying home to enlist.

When the ambulance had gone, I got down and out of habit glanced around, looking for a porter to take my valise, and then picked it up to carry it myself.

It was difficult to find a taxi, and the streets were cluttered with people, either coming from the port or heading toward it. The journey took twice, three times as long to accomplish as it had when I'd come over from England. And then finally, I reached the harbor.

Ships of every size and description lay at anchor disgorging men and equipment, others were steaming in or out of the port, heading across the Channel. Columns of troops were marching toward me, while orderlies were carrying wounded down to the quay to be taken aboard.

I looked up and in the distance saw a tall man wearing an officer's cap over his unruly red hair giving orders to a young lieutenant.

"Rory?" I shouted and hurried after him. But he was gone before I could catch him up. Was it Rory? Cousin Kenneth's eldest son and his heir? I stood there shaken. I wasn't surprised to find him here, on his way to the fighting. But to see him marching off toward those guns, was entirely different. Wrenching—

An officer came up to me. "Miss? You shouldn't be here."

"I must take a ship to England. I want to go home. I was caught in Paris, you see, when war broke out."

"I doubt it's possible. Every bit of space is given over to the wounded. I'd advise you to find an hotel, and wait there until something can be arranged."

And then he was gone.

I am seldom at a loss about what to do next. But this was so far out of my ordinary world that I couldn't think straight. And then I saw an hotel sign and went inside. It was going to be a long day, and my valise was growing heavier by the minute in my hands. I needed to find a room.

But there was none to be had. The city was crammed with men, and those who were wounded but still ambulatory had taken every available space. I'd lost count of hotels by the time I walked into another one and saw two officers just settling their accounts. I rushed to the desk and bespoke the room before someone else could.

One of the officers turned, looked down at me, and then exclaimed, "Good God! Lady Elspeth? What in the—what the devil are you doing in Calais?"

It was Jeremy Martin-Ward, whose sister I'd stayed with in Surrey for a lovely weekend.

"Jeremy? I've been caught in Paris all this time. I'm desperate to get back to England."

"Aren't we all?" his companion said. "I don't believe we've been introduced."

Jeremy ignored him, turning to the desk clerk, already bombarded with requests for the room he'd just relinquished. *"Cette jeune femme est ma soeur.* Give her my room." Quicker than the eye could follow, a few sous were passed across the desk, and the clerk pocketed them without a trace of expression.

"But, of course, *mon capitaine.* It is understood."

A very different world from the diffident politeness I'd experienced as a guest of the Villards in Paris. I made a note of how things were done now.

Jeremy left, and a porter carried my valise up to the room. It was small and stuffy, and the sheets were suspect. I begged two fresh ones, and the porter promised to bring them up *tout de suite*. I had a few coins in my hand, and the exchange of clean sheets and sous went smoothly.

These people were in the middle of a war, their future uncertain. Who could blame them for making the most of whatever opportunities came their way?

I opened my valise to find a fresh handkerchief and blinked in surprise when I saw on top of my belongings a square of heavy brown paper done up with string.

My first thought was that one of the servants at the Villard house had given me a parting gift. Touched, I undid the string, unwrapped the paper, and found myself staring at a painting of a Highland scene, three men in kilts standing in the foreground of a castle.

It was very poorly done, this painting, and the pattern of the tartans was wrong. I couldn't think of a single clan they represented. What's more, the castle was more French than Scots. Pretty and romantic, not the rugged towers and keeps of Scotland.

But then someone in the Villard household must have believed that this was a true representation and one that I would appreciate.

I looked in the folds of the brown paper, but there was no card or letter. Well, that was easily enough remedied, I thought as I wrapped the painting again and retied the string. I'd ask Madeleine when next I wrote to find out who was to be thanked for my gift. I found my handkerchiefs, put everything back in the valise, and set it in the ancient armoire.

Locking the door to my room, I set out on my quest to find a ship for Dover.

A number of stretchers were laid on the road down to the harbor, and the men lying on them looked parched, their bandages black with flies and dried blood. Shocked, I went into the nearest café, found a jug of water, and brought it back. The owner could only give me a single tin cup, but it would have to do. I gave each man a little water, and when the stretcher bearers came to fetch them, moved on to others waiting their turn.

"Why are they lying here like this?" I demanded of an orderly hurrying by.

"The ambulances had to go back, Miss. They couldn't stay. There was nothing else to do but unload the wounded. We're that far behind getting them aboard."

A ship for England could wait. I went back into the café, bought two more jugs of water, and at a small shop next door, I purchased a leather satchel, the sort men used to carry their work tools. I made more trips to that café and others, and there never seemed to be enough water for all those wounded.

Before the next convoy of ambulances went back again, I was ready. I found a tough Glaswegian sergeant driving one, and by the time I had finished talking to him, I'd earned a seat in his ambulance back to the sorting station where the wounded were collected. The drive was shocking, through shattered landscapes, broken buildings, pitted roads, that bore no resemblance to the villages that must once have stood here. *Such waste,* I thought. And where were the people? Long since become refugees on the long hard road to a precarious safety, the driver told me.

We came to a temporary aid station. I thought I could smell the front lines beyond—sweat and blood and dirty bodies and fear. The bombardment was deafening, and through it, the sounds of rifle fire, machine guns, screams. Explosion after explosion rocked us, sending up great showers of earth in the distance where the fighting was fiercest.

I had a rough idea where we were, having looked at that map in Henri's study. Ypres was somewhere ahead. It lay in a shallow bowl, rising land on three sides, including Passchendaele Ridge. I had the sinking feeling that all was not going well, that the Germans were pushing hard and the British were barely holding on.

I got out and began looking for wounded. Instead I found pockets of soldiers who had fallen back after days in the line, and I gave them all the water I had. They were so grateful, as if I'd given them something of great value.

Moving on, I found the aid station in what had been a small village square. No one sent me away when I offered to help.

Clouds came over the sun, bringing blessed relief from the late summer heat, and for a moment I sat down on an overturned stone that looked as if it had fallen from the cornice at the top of a house. Behind me orderlies and an overworked doctor did what they could for the wounded. I had never seen so much blood, and it sickened me to look at the wounds, terrible, destructive to bone and flesh and spirit. I had already helped where I could for hours, it seemed, running and fetching, doing what untrained hands could do. My pale cream traveling suit was dusty and stained with blood, filthy at the knees from kneeling.

I thought to myself I'd never seen such courage as these men showed. I'd grown up on the tales of feuds and clan warfare, of The Bruce, who became king, and William Wallace, who had been killed by another king, of Bonnie Prince Charlie and Culloden Moor. Those had been rousing accounts of battles and bravery, faithlessness and daring deeds. This was different. This was blood and broken bodies and men who held on against incredible odds, and then collapsed in exhaustion. I turned away so no one could see me and I cried for their anguish. And then I stood up to ask again what I might do. I was sent to hold the hands of the dying. It was the most heartbreaking thing I'd ever done.

Coming back to my cornice a little later, I could feel the weariness in my very bones. Lady Elspeth Douglas, who could dance all night and be fresh the next morning, who could play tennis all afternoon and then dine with friends or attend a musical evening with more dancing, found there were limits to her strength that she had not even dreamed of. It was shocking.

A man came up to where I was sitting, angry words preceding him. "Young woman? What the hell are you doing here?"

I turned, and his anger was arrested as he stared at me. "Lady Elspeth? My good God, what are you doing in *France?*"

It was Peter Gilchrist, head of one of the larger septs or branches of his clan. I had known him as a child but hadn't seen him in years. His face was streaked with black smoke and dried blood, not his own, surely. His uniform was ripped in several places, and even his boots were the worse for wear from clambering about over the rubble. I had never seen eyes so haunted and tired—except here, where it was a badge of honor.

"We're retreating. From Ypres. You shouldn't be here."

"I know. I wanted to bring water to the men. I hadn't realized how far I'd come." A ranging shell fell nearby, and Peter Gilchrist caught me by the arm and pulled me roughly behind a high wall, all that was left of a garden, the ground behind it chewed into mud and debris. I saw a single geranium blossom under my feet, its white petals bruised and torn. *Like the men,* I thought.

Another ranging shell came over, this time raining debris and earth all over us, and I heard men screaming somewhere on the far side of the wall.

"Come on, we've got to move," Peter said, getting to his feet and dragging me up as well. "This way. The next one will catch us if we don't."

He turned and shouted to one of his sergeants, and men raced back down what had been a road, now littered with everything from earth to a soldier's shoe. Others had caught up the stretchers, and the doctor ran alongside, worry on his face as he tried to stop the bleeding of the man he was treating.

I felt useless, helpless. But I could run, and I did, staying clear of the men fighting a ferocious rearguard action, staying clear of the stretcher bearers, taking care not to fall and make trouble for everyone.

I don't think I've run so far since my school days, playing sports in the afternoon.

Out of breath, my throat so dry it hurt, I kept Peter in sight.

And then we were out of range. But not before I'd seen that garden wall blown to bits not minutes after we'd left its shelter.

We dropped where we were, to catch our breath. Peter saw to his men and then came to me. "You must get back," he said urgently. "We could still be overrun, or shelled. And there have been no ambulances for the past two hours. What am I to do with you, Lady Elspeth?" There was despair in his voice.

"I'll be all right. If I didn't have vapors when those shells came in, I won't have them now. Just tell me where I can stay out of the way—or what I can do to help?"

He looked around. Down the street from where we stood was a ruined church, one wall and a doorway still standing, the rest only a mountain of stone where the nave and sanctuary had been.

"There. Stay in that space between the wall and the church door. It should be safe enough. But if you see us running, don't wait for me. Just follow, fast as you can."

Someone had found the time to brew hot water over a tiny flame, and I still had my tin cup. The corporal, a young Highlander with hair as red as Cousin Kenneth's own, came shyly up to me, offering me a little of his tea. I was going to refuse, and then I saw that he meant for me to have it, and I took it, drinking it gratefully.

"Ye're a Douglas," the corporal said, no idea that I had a title before my name. "Any kin to Major Rory Douglas?"

"A cousin," I said. "Is he still alive? Is he all right?"

"He's well. Last time I saw. But he's lost a brother."

My heart turned over. Not Bruce, who played the piano so beautifully and had a devil of merriment in his gray eyes.

"I didna' hear which one," he went on before I could ask. "But I served under yon Major. He's a verra' fine officer. If I see him again, I'll tell him a cousin was asking after him."

And then he was gone. They say a Scot will search the world for his kin, and this man—boy—had done just that, giving me comfort and telling me the news, as he would to his own cousin in London or Canada or Australia. I was touched.

It was nearly dark when Peter came back to where I was sitting. The guns were silent now all along the Front, and I took it that the Germans were resting as well. But for what? Tomorrow's attack?

He leaned his dark head back against the stone arch of the church door, moved to a slightly more comfortable place, and sighed.

I'd seen his care for his men, and in their turn, their respect for him, their trust in him. I'd seen his concern for his wounded, his awareness of everything happening around him. He'd found time for me, in the midst of a major withdrawal, and tired as he was, he still had hope. Hope that this was a temporary reversal of fortune, and that in due course, he'd soon be retaking lost territory. Most of all, I could see how the boy I'd known, a friend of Cousin Bruce's, had grown into this man. There was something about him that I found myself liking more than I should.

"Dear God, what a day. The French have turned the German Army back on us. It's a holding action now, trying to keep them from breaking south here along the coast. They won't retreat back into Belgium. They came to fight, and they will."

"But surely you're outnumbered," I said, remembering the taxis of Paris. They needed taxis here too—desperately. The British Army was scattered across the Empire, and the Expeditionary Force, although made up of tested men, couldn't multiply itself overnight.

"We are indeed outnumbered. We came to protect against a flanking movement as the main body of the German Army made for the Marne Valley. From what I hear, they came very close to taking Paris."

I told him what I'd seen, a regiment in Renaults.

He chuckled appreciatively. "That was a clever move, I must say. I wish we could expect rescue as easily. But as it is . . ." His voice trailed off. "I have no food to offer you. But you must be dreadfully hungry."

I thought of the night I'd gone out with Alain and eaten simple but delicious food at a café where the ordinary people of Paris went to dine. Where we wouldn't be seen by anyone we knew and cause gossip.

"I must admit I could do with a little cheese and a heel of one of those lovely crusty loaves."

"God, yes." A silence fell. "I haven't seen you since your father died. I'm sorry. I know how close you were."

"Were you at his funeral?" I hadn't seen him. I'd been in a state of shock and hardly knew where I was.

"I came in at the last minute. The train from London was late, and I had no chance to speak to you before the service. Afterward, you were in seclusion."

I'd given instructions that I didn't want to see anyone. There had been so many mourners that I'd been overcome by their grief, and I'd needed time to face my own. "It was kind of you to come," I managed to say, and then, to shut out the painful memories that were rushing in, I added, "And you? What has happened in your life, besides the war?"

"I lost my father as well. But you must have heard that. I chose the Army, as he had done."

"Who's minding the clan?"

"My younger brother. The lame one. He'll do better than I ever shall."

"I doubt that."

"No, seriously, there's so much to be done. And I'm not there to do it."

"And you've never married?" He was five years my elder. I wouldn't have been surprised to hear he'd taken a wife, if only to assure an heir. Heirs mattered in our families. I understood that very well.

"No. There was a girl I rather liked in Canada, when the regiment was posted there, but nothing came of it." He glanced down at the ring on my finger. "You?"

For some reason I couldn't tell him I was promised, although of course nothing was official. Not until Alain could speak to my cousin. I was afraid to utter the words aloud, for fear of tempting the gods of war. Too many *ifs*. If Alain came through safely, if my cousin could be persuaded. If we were both of the same mind, Alain and I, after a long separation.

Instead, I said, "Not from want of trying on my cousin Kenneth's part."

He smiled, a flash of white teeth in the shadows. "If he could see you now, he'd marry you to the first man who crossed his threshold, just to get you out of here." He was quiet for a moment, then he said, "You should have stayed in Paris. It was safer than coming to Calais."

I shook my head. "I had to stay until my friend had her child. I'd promised her that. Afterward, I felt a surprising surge of homesickness. I had to find my way to England. Or at least try."

"You'll never get out through Calais. They can't even take the walking wounded. No room."

"I've seen them, filling the hotels."

"Yes. Do you need a blanket? I'll see if I can find one."

"I'm all right. The stone is still warm."

"It can be quite chilly at night. After the heat of the

day." He moved his head again and then turned to see what it was that was making him uncomfortable. "A saint's foot," he said, touching the protruding toe. "Who do you suppose the saint is? I can't make out his symbol." He leaned back. "French, no doubt." I thought he might have fallen asleep, for he was silent after that. And then without opening his eyes, he said, "I've got to make rounds, speak to the sentries." Rising, stretching wearily, he strode away.

Half an hour later he was back. He'd found a blanket, although it smelled strongly of horse, and he laid it across my lap. "You'll be grateful for this later. There's no more tea, sad to say. We're nearly out of ammunition as well. If we aren't resupplied or relieved soon, we're done for. And we need to get the wounded back. Two more have died."

There was an intimacy sitting here together in the darkness, his feet on the other side of mine, my skirts touching his boots. I could put out my hand and touch his. As if he realized it, he drew back a little. "Should I try to find somewhere more comfortable? Are you all right?"

"You need to sleep, not worry about me." I passed the blanket to him, to put behind his head. After that, we both slept a little, though not a restful sleep. He was gone several times on his rounds, and once when I awoke, I was lying down, the blanket covering me, stiff and thirsty but not cold.

I was still asleep when I felt a rumble through the stones beneath me. At first I thought the guns had started up again and then I realized the sound was coming from the opposite direction. Peter appeared just then. "Word has come. They've got ambulances and lorries to take us back. Come on, I want you in the first of them."

We got the wounded loaded, then most of the men on board one or another of the vehicles. The rest would fall back slowly, covering our retreat.

At the last minute Peter leapt into the ambulance beside me, barely space for two and now holding three. I was jammed against his chest, and he had put one arm back behind my head to make a little more room. "Sorry," he said as my hair caught on one of his coat buttons. "There's literally no other seat. I've been ordered back with the bulk of my men. Another officer has been sent forward to lead the rear guard."

I was grateful for his presence beside me, sparing me the worst of the buffeting and bruising that followed. We jolted and bounced, aiming for speed, putting some distance between us and what lay behind, the shuttered beams of the ambulance headlamps helping us not at all but soon touching the grim faces of columns of troops moving up to take our place. British troops, marching to fill the gap and hold on a little longer. They went silently, and I thought, *They know what they will be facing.* They can't help but see the cost, carried in the ambulances.

I watched them with sadness. So much courage . . .

Our driver, hunched over his wheel, the muscles of his bare arms—for he had taken off his tunic—bunched into cords as he fought to control it.

"We need to stop," he said to Peter soon after we'd encountered the relief column. "The wounded will need to be looked to."

"Another five miles," Peter told him. "We must make five more miles, long as our column is."

I was reminded again of the taxis streaking out of Paris, but this time it was a full retreat in whatever vehicles the Army could muster. I didn't think the new men could hold in face of German determination, any more than Peter's men had. But they would try.

The driver swore in Gaelic, pointing ahead.

Peter Gilchrist said quietly, "Just as well we can't understand what he's saying."

I could, for my sins.

"He declares he sees steam ahead. Trains."

Captain Gilchrist leaned forward to stare through the dust-blurred windscreen. "By God, I think he's right!"

"Did you never learn the Gaelic?" I asked.

"My father was in the Scots Guards. I grew up in England. There was no one to teach me, although what I picked up from his men was more useful in a brawl than in polite society." He had been as tired as I was, but now he seemed to come alive again, knowing his men would be safe for a time buoying him as he watched the lead ambulance thread its way through the companies of soldiers jumping out of the trains and hurrying to fall in.

"It's going to take the rest of the night to untangle this chaos," he said and reached down to open his door. "But thank God for it. Stay here. I'll make a space on the train for you as soon as I have things in hand. Promise me not to wander off. God knows when there will be another train. Not with Germans on our heels."

I promised, and he got out. The colder morning air, coming off the sea, swept into his place, and I shivered.

I watched as he and the other officers sorted out the new men and began to load the wounded, the retreating forces with us falling in to lend a hand. They were making good progress when a Major came to the side of our lead ambulance.

"Turn around as soon as you can and start back toward the fighting. There will be more casualties before the sun sets today."

And then he saw me.

"Who the hell is this?" he demanded of the driver in Gaelic.

"A lass who has been helping the wounded. The Captain was sending her back to Calais."

"Who are you and what are you doing with the Army?" he said, bending lower to see me better.

He'd spoken in French, thinking I must be a refugee—or worse, a spy—and I answered in English.

"Lady Elspeth Douglas. I was on my way to England, and I got separated from my party in the chaos."

I was sure I looked more like a drudge than an aristocrat, for he hadn't removed his cap until I gave my name.

"This will never do. There's no place in Calais for a woman."

"There's no place for me up there," I said. "Captain Gilchrist—"

"Captain Gilchrist's duties at the moment do not allow

for dealing with refugees. Come with me." He hurried around the ambulance to open my door, saying to the driver, "You have your orders," as he handed me down.

And the ambulance pulled out. I saw that others were turning as well as soon as they were empty, and the soldiers from the train were starting to form up behind them.

I was led to a staff car waiting by the siding, motor running. The smoke from the engines was making my eyes water, and I couldn't see Captain Gilchrist anywhere.

"Sergeant," my companion said to his driver, "keep her here. Out of sight. Do you understand?"

"Sir, yes, sir," the man replied smartly.

And then the Major was gone. I sat in the back of the staff car, watching the scene before me turn to order, hoping Peter would find me before the Major returned. But in the darkness I could hardly tell one officer from another. And luck had deserted me. The Major was back again before very long, taking his seat beside me, his lieutenant reduced to sitting in the front with the sergeant.

Without a word we drove away.

I found myself wishing I could have said good-bye to Peter Gilchrist. But the Major was right about one thing, he was too busy to play at nursemaid, and if I stayed, I could get him killed as he tried to juggle my safety and that of his men.

For the guns had opened up again, first the Germans and then the nearer salvos as the English answered. Peter Gilchrist's night was not over.

• *Chapter Three* •

As we left Ypres behind and drove through the flat land south of it, dawn broke, clouds on the horizon lingering but still promising another hot day ahead.

The Major began to quiz me.

Who was I? Where had I been? Why had I come to France? How had I got separated from my party? On and on the questions. I was short of sleep and short of patience, but I answered them with courtesy.

"There is a valise in an hotel in Calais. Mine, if it is still there. I should like to see if it is, and make myself presentable before boarding a ship."

But the Major shook his head. "You aren't crossing at Calais. No. I'll send someone to find your valise if I can."

"I shouldn't stay in France," I reminded him.

"I'm well aware of that, Lady Elspeth."

At that moment the lieutenant, in the front, said something in Gaelic. I caught it but said nothing.

"She's related to the Major, sir. Must be."

That put a different light on the matter, apparently.

My Major said, "Thank you," to his lieutenant, then gave the matter some thought. Finally he said, "There's a convoy of lorries on their way to Rouen, or there should be. We're bringing in supplies through the port, and you're more likely to find a space for England there. I'll send a pass with you."

And then, as if he'd disposed of this thorny problem, he turned to his lieutenant and began making lists of what was needed in the north and what he had arranged to be done. The lieutenant, a notebook on his knee, was writing quickly, trying to keep up with the spate of orders and comments as we bounced and slid on the war-torn road.

I settled into a corner, tried to sleep, but found myself feeling bereft. Alone in a strange, cold world.

Calais was no better, possibly even worse. The Major sent his sergeant into the hotel I pointed out, and the man came back a quarter of an hour later with my valise. By this time the Major had gone on, leaving me with the young lieutenant.

They flagged down one of the convoy of lorries forming up for the journey to Rouen, and I was put aboard, in the front with the driver, my valise stowed. From his notebook, the lieutenant took three sheets of paper, passed one to the driver, one to me, and the third he held.

"Those are your instructions, Corporal. She is not to leave the lorry before you reach the port at Rouen. Understood?"

"Sir, yes."

To me he said, "That's your pass for Rouen. You mustn't lose it. And this"—he handed the third sheet to the driver—"this is her passage chit. Don't let her have it until you've handed her over to the port authorities."

He hesitated, then took off his cap, his fair hair already dark with sweat. "I'm so sorry, Lady Elspeth, but your room had been given over to others, and there was no place for you to freshen up. I apologize as well for the Major, but he has a great deal on his mind just now, as you'll understand. He has your best interests at heart, but we're at war, and he can't take needless risks with civilian lives."

It was so kind of him. I felt a rush of sympathy for him, having to endure the Major's bad nature. "Thank you, Lieutenant, for your concern. I know how trying I've been. I won't give you or the Major any more cause for concern. And if you should see Captain Gilchrist again, will you give him my gratitude and that of my family for seeing me safely to the trains?"

He smiled, nodded to me, and was gone. I was certain he'd forgot me before he'd walked twenty yards, for his notebook was out and he was busy studying it, dodging the wounded, the relief columns, and the refugees with the ease of long practice. *Quite a comedown for Lady Elspeth Douglas,* I thought wryly, who was accustomed to young men clamoring for the next dance or begging to take me in to supper.

And then he was lost to sight as we turned toward Rouen. I stowed away my pass very carefully and settled down for the journey. The driver was taciturn, a small dark Welshman, polite enough but not very happy to have a passenger. I could smell fresh baked bread, an onion, and what I thought were sausages, very likely his lunch, from just behind my seat.

I hadn't eaten since I left Paris. How long ago was that? But even as my stomach twisted in pangs of hunger, I couldn't ask my companion if I could share his meal. Who knew when he would get another? There were refugees along the road here, faces drawn and weary, shops closed and shuttered in the villages, farm gates barred, everyone holding on to what he had, for fear there would be no more.

Some miles out of Rouen, my driver reached over into the back and pulled out a small canvas holdall.

I still had my tin cup in my pocket, and I hoped he had wine or tea or even the strong French coffee as well.

To my surprise, he offered to share with me, but I took only enough of the bread and sausage to keep me from feeling faint, and a little of the tea. He ate hungrily, and I knew I'd done the right thing.

It was late afternoon before we reached Rouen, famous for its cathedral, its long history, Joan of Arc, and its very popular racecourse, closed now for the duration. Riders and punters all gone off to war.

We made our way to the port, the line of lorries echoing loudly in the narrow streets of the town, causing those walking along to stop and stare at us. Two nuns made the sign of the cross, and a little girl, clinging to her mother's skirts, began to cry. How long before they were inured to war, and took no notice of British lorries?

The officer in charge of the port, we were told, had come down with an attack of malaria. No one had taken his place, and there was chaos everywhere I looked.

My Welsh driver looked at me, said, "This is the port," and handed me my orders. "You'll have to fend for yourself, lass, and if you get into any trouble, don't look to me." It was said with more kindliness than it sounded.

"I want nothing more than to sail for England. As soon as may be. The Major is not alone in wanting me out of France."

He looked around him. "They're saying in London the war will be over by Christmas." He shrugged. "I'm not sure I believe them, standing here."

For the commercial port had become an armed camp, and it was taking on an air of permanence even as we watched, or so it seemed to me.

He turned and went to join the other lorry drivers waiting for instructions.

I had learned much since I left Paris.

I walked smartly down to the port, found a man to carry my valise, and after a few well-placed bribes, I found myself on board the *Leviathan,* given the third officer's cramped cabin. And as the ship plowed through the darkness, down the Seine and out into the rougher waters of the Channel, I set about making myself presentable for my arrival in England. I'd been right to bring as little as possible from Paris. Whatever would I have done with a trunk? I wondered wryly. Though wrinkled, the clothing in my valise was clean, fresh enough, and quite suitable for landing in Portsmouth. That was all that mattered.

It was a measure of how tired I was that I hadn't noticed that the painting was missing from my valise. I was just putting up my hair when it occurred to me. I turned and looked through my possessions, even though I knew it wasn't there.

What I did find, to my surprise, caught in a silk scarf, were several specks of what looked rather like tiny flakes of paint. They were the same blue used in one of the kilts.

But who would steal such an ugly painting, leaving behind my jewelry? I couldn't fathom it, but I was really beyond caring.

I was about to fall asleep when another thought struck me. I had no idea where that painting had come from. I'd just assumed it had been meant as a gift, the giver thinking that the scene would appeal to me.

But what if it wasn't?

A knock at the cabin door distracted me, and I found a rating outside with a covered tray. I could smell soup and meat, and there was bread; I could see the outline of it under the serviette.

"With the compliments of Mr. Thomas," the rating said, and I struggled to remember who that was. The third officer?

"Thank Mr. Thomas for his kindness," I said, and took the tray from him.

There *was* soup, and with it roasted potatoes and several

slices of ham with cabbage. Seaman's fare, but I ate it all and was grateful. I must have dropped off to sleep again soon after finishing the meal, for when I woke up some time later, the tray had been taken away and a blanket had been pulled up across my shoulders as I lay in the berth. Somehow it had wedged itself around me, protecting my back against the ship's roll and pitch, feeling remarkably like the comfort of arms.

I realized instantly what had awakened me—a difference in the motion of the ship. I turned off the lamp and looked out the porthole. We were just coming into Portsmouth.

I had decided early on that once we had docked in Portsmouth I would go on to Cornwall. Most of the wardrobe I'd taken with me to Paris was still there, of course, and I needed something more appropriate to London than what I had with me, mainly travel clothes. Hardly suitable for dinners or even afternoon calls. But by the time I'd disembarked, I had changed my mind, sending a telegram to Cornwall and giving the staff there my instructions for what to send to me in London in care of my cousin Kenneth's house.

That done, I nearly changed my mind again. It would be tempting to go directly to Cornwall, shut myself behind the walls of my stone house overlooking the sea, and put this wretched war out of my mind. I'd seen its reality, the terrible wounds men and their weapons could inflict on one another, men dying by the roadside or in the meager shelter of a ruined town. But there was no running away.

Not for me. The question was, what was I going to do with myself?

I touched the ring on my finger, wondering how long it would be before I heard news of Alain.

Why had I told Peter Gilchrist that I wasn't engaged? I could have explained—I could have told him that the ring was a token of Alain's promise to speak to my cousin as soon as he could.

Instead I'd denied any commitment, and more to the point, I'd taken pleasure in Peter's company. I could still feel his arm around me, his body breaking the worst of the ambulance's jolting ride.

I tried to convince myself that it was the war, it was the frightfulness of being shelled, of working with the wounded and dying, the unsettling experience of being in the company of men without the presence of a chaperone or a male member of my family.

I'd just stepped out into the street after sending my telegram when I nearly collided with a man hurrying toward the post office. He was familiar, I'd seen him before, but I couldn't remember where.

It wasn't until I had reached the railway station that I remembered. He'd had the seat next to mine on the journey from Paris.

The train north was crowded and very slow, for we were often held up as troop trains hurtled past. And when I reached London at last, I discovered that my cousin's house—once my father's—had been shut up for the duration, only a skeleton staff in residence. I asked the housekeeper to watch for my trunk, went up to my room, and took away some clothing to be going on with.

Before leaving, I asked for news of my cousins, and the housekeeper told me, "My lady, there's been no word about Mr. Bruce. His lordship did write to say the Captain is all right. We pray for both of them every night."

As I myself did.

I went to Brown's Hotel, but Reception and the lounge were jammed with people in search of rooms. It was my first taste of what was to come, if the war lasted beyond Christmas.

On my third try, I managed to find a room, and that afternoon I went to call on one of my father's oldest friends. Gerald Hamilton was a slim man of medium height, with new lines in his face that told me what the past few weeks had cost him. He had taken his seat in the House of Lords as soon as he'd come into his title, and he had urged my father to do the same. Speed consumed him instead, and yet the two men had remained firm friends.

We talked about my father for a few minutes, and then I told Lord Hamilton what I had seen in France, leaving out my two days along the road to Ypres.

"I want to do something to help," I said in conclusion. "I need advice, and I don't know where else to turn."

He considered me for a moment. "Your cousin would want you to go home. And as your father's friend, I'd advise that as well."

"How can I hide in Scotland from this war? My cousins are fighting in France. I've been told—I was told that one of them could be dead." My voice nearly broke as I finished.

"My dear girl, I hadn't heard—"

Before I quite knew what I was saying, I interrupted him. "I want to join Queen Alexandra's Imperial Military Nursing Service."

He stared at me. "Are you quite serious? What will your cousin say? What would your father think?"

"My father would tell you that I can speak for myself," I countered, avoiding answering the question directly.

But Lord Hamilton wouldn't hear of it. In the end, I thanked him and left soon thereafter, promising to consider his advice to go to Scotland.

Outside I stood there wondering where that sudden decision to join the Nursing Service had come from. I knew nothing about nursing, nothing about the qualifications or the training. More to the point, I had no idea how to go about finding out. But I already understood very well the need for trained care for the wounded.

A stream of people coming and going into the House of Lords were stepping around me, and I realized that I was blocking the doorway.

I walked on, deep in thought, and as I came into Trafalgar Square, I glimpsed a young woman in the distinctive blue uniform of the Service. I ran after her, causing heads to turn, and called, "Sister!"

She stopped, looking around, and as I caught her up, I said with a smile, "I'm so sorry for shouting after you. But you see, I'd like to know how to join the Service. And no one will tell me." It wasn't precisely true that *no one* would tell me—I'd only spoken to Lord Hamilton—but that was neither here nor there.

The woman returned my smile. "I met with the same obstinacy," she said. "But I was determined, you see."

"Come and have tea with me," I suggested, "and tell me what I need to know."

I gave her my name—Elspeth Douglas—as we walked down The Strand and found a respectable hotel serving tea, saying nothing about my title. I don't precisely know why I hadn't given it. For fear she would tell me the Service was not for me, as Lord Hamilton had done? Or for fear of putting her off? Whatever the reason, it was done. And indeed, taking me for someone very like herself, of good family and background, she seemed eager to talk about her own experiences.

She told me her name was Sister Margaret Fielding, and that she came from Norfolk, where her parents were still living. "They've decided to speak to me again," she added wryly. "At first they treated me as if I no longer existed. Which hurt, you know, but I refused to let that stop me. Of course, my sister had been a suffragette, much to their dismay. Both daughters such a disappointment. Luckily my brother chose the church, which has made them very happy."

Even while I was laughing with her, I could imagine Cousin Kenneth not speaking to me, if he found out. Still, Queen Alexandra's Imperial Military Nursing Service had made nursing the wounded a respectable and respected occupation, with royal approval.

Another thought struck me. Would I need his permission to join? Would he give it? He was my guardian until I was thirty.

Something I must consider carefully.

"What was their objection?" I asked, pouring our tea.

"It's what you must do that distressed them," Sister Fielding explained. "Washing the bodies of strange men, attending doctors as they work with bloody or disgusting wounds, carrying bedpans—you can see it's hardly the best occupation for an innocent young woman. But I *contribute* something, and that matters more to me than the onerous duties I must perform. My brother is in the Army, a chaplain, you know, and I think of him often, hoping that if he's ever wounded, he'll be cared for by someone who is trained to treat him."

Half an hour later, we parted outside the hotel, and I had the information I needed to start my search.

Rather pleased with my resourcefulness, I walked back to my hotel. But the euphoria soon wore off, and I began to wonder if I was truly interested in nursing, or if Lord Hamilton's reaction to the very idea had brought out the stubbornness that my father and I were known for.

Would my father have approved of what I was about to do? Did I have the courage to see it through, as Sister Fielding had done? The training alone was formidable.

The only answer I could give myself was *France*. I *had* seen those torn bodies, the orderlies rushing here and there to help where they could, doctors harassed and exhausted, working with a calmness of a surgeon in his own surgical theater, shutting out everything else but what their fingers were doing as they raced time to save another life.

What if it were Henri—or Alain—or Rory—or Peter—who lay severely wounded and in need of my care? Could I keep my head and tend them without crying or feeling faint? Could I hold them down as the doctor removed a limb?

I shuddered at the thought, but my answer was *Yes*, for their sakes. I could.

I don't know if I dreamed or not, but in the morning the bedclothes were in disarray. If I had, it was surely of Alain. Not of a British officer who kept me warm against the night's chill and got me to safety. I had no reason to dream of *him*.

When I went down to dinner, I encountered three of my friends. They were in uniform and the Honorable Freddie Huntington told me he'd just proposed to Alicia Terrill. We toasted his happiness while he expounded on his good fortune, for she was very popular.

Turning to me, he said, "And you, Lady Elspeth? Does that ring mean you've also become engaged?"

They teased me until I told them that it was a family heirloom. Freddie was something of a gossip and a friend of Rory's as well. I could just imagine the news reaching Cousin Kenneth's ears before Alain could come to England. It would be the worst possible thing.

But their banter was a reminder to remove it before I interviewed with the Nursing Service.

• *Chapter Four* •

THE NEXT MORNING, I SET out on my rounds.

The first person I encountered was Timothy Howard, of the War Office. He was on his way to speak to the Prime Minister, and we stopped in the street to talk. Before we parted, I asked, "What's the news from France?"

If anyone knew what was happening, he did.

"I was hoping you could tell me. I think we've stopped the German forward advance on both fronts, but now I'm terrified they'll dig in and this will become a stalemate," he said grimly. "And that would be the worst possible thing for everyone. The French can't push the Germans back across the Frontier, and nor can we. What was the general mood in France?"

I told him everything I'd seen, and he whistled. "You should have stayed in Paris. It was too dangerous to try for a port."

"I know that now. I didn't then. Besides, I needed to

come home. Timothy, do you know a Captain Gilchrist? Peter Gilchrist?"

"Yes, of course I do. We were in school together. Please don't tell me he's dead."

"He was alive a few days ago," I said, and explained.

"Well, you were in the best of hands, I can tell you that. You've had quite an adventure," he added, admiration in his voice. "But you could manage, if anyone could."

I had, but I realized now how lucky I'd been as well.

"Timothy, I want to be a nurse."

"A nurse? Good Lord, Lady Elspeth. Are you quite serious?"

"Quite serious," I replied.

"Well." He thought about it. "Speak to your cousin first. You're his ward, you'll need his permission to get into the training program. Besides, if the war ends by Christmas, you'll have gone through rigorous training for nothing. Have you considered that?"

"It's a very good point," I agreed.

"Where are you staying? I understood the London house was closed."

"In an hotel," I told him. "Before I was given a room I had to tell Reception that I'd come to London to see my cousins off to France," I added wryly. Unaccompanied young women were not welcomed in good hotels.

"I'm not surprised. Lodgings are springing up all over. But they aren't for the likes of you."

Eager to change the subject now, I said, harking back to his comment about training, "You don't really believe that this war will be over by Christmas." I'd met Kaiser Wilhelm at a formal dinner in Berlin while traveling with my cousins. He hadn't struck me as the sort to back down.

"For God's sake, keep this to yourself. But I think we're in for a long struggle. I've advised the Army to take every man they can lay hands on. We're going to need them."

Shocked, I said, "Truly?"

"Truly. So get yourself to Scotland and stay there out of harm's way for the duration. London will be a madhouse. You can't begin to imagine how grim it's going to be. We're already looking at short supplies of food. Your father would be out of his grave and haunting all of us, if we encouraged you in this wild idea."

I smiled. "Don't worry about me, Timothy. I've also been toying with the idea of going down to Cornwall rather than travel to Scotland. Perhaps I should do just that."

He gave me a wary glance. "Lady Elspeth," he began, having known me for quite some time.

I affected my most innocent look. Since he couldn't very well call me a liar to my face, he had to believe me.

Finally he said, "Please. Don't do anything rash."

I promised, and he had to be satisfied. I watched him walk away, thinking that two people now had tried to discourage me from taking up nursing. It was a measure of what? Their belief that I was too fragile to attempt it? Or that it could reflect poorly on my social standing? Possibly even spoil my chances of making a good marriage? A loss of innocence?

I sighed. But I'd also learned something from Timothy

and Lord Hamilton. If I wanted to pursue this idea of training to be a nurse, I had to do it quietly, without fanfare.

The first order of business was to find respectable lodgings where no one would recognize me once I was wearing a uniform. For one thing, I couldn't remain in an hotel of the sort my father would have chosen to stay in; I was all too likely to run into people I knew. I couldn't come and go at all hours without attracting gossip. Word would very soon reach my cousin's ears.

But London seemed to be cheek by jowl with people on the same errand. Every respectable lodging house I approached was already full.

Then, as luck would have it, I saw another young woman in the uniform of Queen Alexandra's Imperial Military Nursing Service, and once more I boldly accosted her as she was about to cross the street.

When I'd finished telling her what I wanted, she smiled. "I've just heard from a friend that a woman called Mrs. Hennessey in Kensington has turned her house into lodgings for young women of good character who are training as nurses."

I got Mrs. Hennessey's direction and thanked Sister Keyes, before hurrying off.

Mrs. Hennessey lived in a large house in Kensington, and she came to the door herself when I knocked. I liked her at once. A pleasant, middle-aged woman, she invited me into the downstairs flat where she herself lived, and asked if I'd already qualified as a Sister.

I gave her my best smile. "I've just come to London to begin my training," I said.

"Which hospital, my dear?"

"Whichever one will take me on," I said, unwilling to lie to her any more than I needed to do, under the circumstances.

"Go to St. Helen's, my dear. I hear they have the best program. Scottish, are you?"

"Yes, from north of Edinburgh." I, who had always taken pride in my title and my lineage, was suddenly finding it a problem. People seemed delighted to help Elspeth Douglas on her way. But everyone who knew Lady Elspeth had been intent on bundling me off to Scotland and safety.

"My late husband had a dear friend who lived in Stirling. I think he would be happy if I took in a Scottish lass."

After we'd had tea, she showed me to the flat with a vacancy. "There are three young women already living here, but there's still room for two more. You should fit in very nicely." She saw my hesitation and said with regret, "It's all I have at the moment."

Used to rooms three times the size of the entire flat, I tried to think what to say. There were five bedrooms not even as large as my mother's dressing room, and then a sitting room shared by all five of us. I could feel the walls closing in as I stood there in the middle of the floor and tried to tell myself I could manage.

"Yes, I'll take the fourth bedroom," I said before I could change my mind. It had two windows, making it seem less claustrophobic than the other choice.

She led me back downstairs where we worked out the details, and then with a flourish she handed over a key.

"There is one rule," she told me. "I don't allow any male over the age of ten up these stairs. If your father or brother or cousin or fiancé comes to see you, you will meet him downstairs in the hall. Is that acceptable to you? I maintain high standards of conduct myself, and I expect my young ladies to do the same."

As I had no father, no brother nor even a cousin, and certainly no fiancé in London, I had no difficulty in agreeing. I was also glad that in such a tiny flat, I wouldn't have to deal with the male relatives of the other residents.

I now had a place to live. It was far more difficult to get myself accepted for training.

When my trunk arrived from Cornwall, I had chosen my most sedate walking dresses for interviews, patterning myself on someone like Sister Fielding. Several times I was tempted to use my title and my father's name, but in the end perseverance paid off. After nearly a week of talking to Matrons, Sisters, a hawk-eyed woman who saw to the financial arrangements, and one doctor who was to assess my steadiness and commitment to this training, I was accepted for the course.

What I hadn't known was that probationers were given the worse possible duties to perform. It was degrading work, but I could see that a young woman who rebelled at cleaning up vomit and excrement and carrying soiled linens to the laundry, who found the old and the dirty and the demented impossible to deal with, would soon be out of the program. And so I rolled up my sleeves, metaphorically as well as literally, and got on with it. I'd been taught from childhood that my title brought with it certain privileges, and that these included certain responsibilities and duties. Was nursing so very different?

If I wished to become a Sister, I must accept the hardships that accompanied that training with whatever grace I could muster.

Once or twice I wondered what my governess would say—she who had taught me to walk with a book on my head, to sit without fidgeting, and to address my elders and my betters in the proper manner—if she could see me cajoling an old and infirm man to eat his pudding. I was comfortable with the aristocracy, I could address an archbishop without flinching, and I knew half the House of Lords. I had made my curtsey to the King and Queen when I came out, and danced with foreign princes. And here I was, washing a woman with bed sores, holding a child with croup as she coughed and gasped for breath, helping a man with one leg to the toilet, and scrubbing surgical theater floors on my hands and knees.

I wore the uniforms I was provided with and was so tired when I got to the flat each night that if I had owned a hundred evening gowns with matching slippers, I'd have never taken them out of the wardrobe. I had books on various medical conditions to read, and when we made rounds with Matron and doctors or watched surgeries, I was expected to answer questions put to us by those whose task it was to decide if the probationers were learning anything at all.

I seldom saw my flatmates. Indeed, we seldom had the same hours free. Bess met me the third morning as I came in from hospital and she was just leaving for it. I learned later that her father was a retired Army Colonel. Mary I met on the weekend, when she had twelve hours off duty and had just slept through ten of them. Diana was always talking about the men in her life, but I soon learned that while she was popular, she was as devoted to nursing as the rest of us.

They accepted me as I was—or seemed to be. A young Scotswoman who wanted to serve her country as much as they did.

We qualified in almost the same order—Bess first, then Mary, and finally Diana. I was not far behind. When the day came that I had earned the title Sister, I felt a surprising surge of pride. I had not inherited this title, I had worked for it. Lady Elspeth Douglas was now Sister Douglas, and her skills were saving lives and comforting the dying.

Amazingly, I had been good at nursing. What I'd seen and done along the road to Ypres had helped me face surgery with an iron will if not an iron stomach. And I had a purpose in this war now. I could do something that counted. My Highland ancestors had never been afraid of a good fight, and they'd won their fair share of them. The women of my family had patched up their clansmen and sent them out to fight again another day.

And here I was, in 1914 doing precisely the same thing. Only there were no pipers to skirl me through the ceremony, but I hoped that the men and the women in my family would be proud of me. Once they recovered from the shock, of course.

All this time, I had heard nothing from Alain. Madeleine had written several times, but I received only one of her letters, and it was filled with worry. Henri had managed to get a single torn and filthy letter through, sending it back with a wounded friend, but after that, silence. She too had heard nothing from Alain. She didn't know whether to go on to the Loire or stay in Paris. But young Henri was thriving, and she wanted above everything for his father to come home and see him. *Once, please, dear God, so that he would know.* I could feel the anguish behind those lines.

Was I promised to a living man? A ghost? My heart refused to believe that Alain was dead. I'd have known, I'd have felt something. Madeleine believed she would know instantly if anything happened to Henri. Would it be the same for me? Had Alain known I was in danger there on the Ypres road?

Why did I feel nothing? Was it because I didn't care enough? Or was he well, tired but alive.

Because of my duties, I had had to remove Alain's ring, but I wore it beneath my uniform on a gold chain. I touched it lightly from time to time, when I needed courage.

Like everyone else, I carefully scanned the British casualty lists in the *Times*. It was depressing, reading the names of men I knew, men I'd laughed and danced and played tennis with, who had been friends since childhood, there amongst the killed, the wounded, the missing. But not the name I watched for. Captain Gilchrist.

I told myself that I had every reason to be grateful to him. But why did I dream sometimes and see his face so clearly?

There were no such lists in England for French casualties. I had to wait for news.

Twice while taking a letter for France to the post office, I'd seen the same man I'd crossed paths with in Portsmouth—the one who had been seated next to me on the train—coming out, and each time he was carrying a parcel wrapped in heavy brown paper and tied with string. The parcels were of different sizes, but so like the one I'd found in my valise in Calais that I felt a surge of suspicion. On the third occasion, I waited until he'd come out of the post office and walked on. Staying well behind him, I followed him through the London streets and waited at the corner when he went into a shop that specialized in old books and fine paintings.

Had he been posting just such a parcel to London when I'd encountered him in Portsmouth after sending my telegram to Cornwall? And that was decidedly odd, because the train would have carried him and the parcel to London so much faster.

When he came out of the shop—without the parcel—I waited until he had disappeared around the next corner and then went inside.

The proprietor was a middle-aged man with a limp

and heavy dark-framed glasses. He peered at me as I came through the door, and I greeted him with all the hauteur of my station, asking if he had any interesting paintings of Scotland that I might buy for my father's birthday.

He showed me several, fine paintings all of them, and I thought perhaps I'd been wrong about the man with the parcel. While pretending to decide whether I liked any of the paintings on offer, I noticed on the edge of his desk several tiny flecks of paint.

Just like the ones I'd seen caught in my silk scarf when I'd searched my valise for the missing parcel.

And in the dust bin behind his desk was a coil of string very like the one around my parcel.

Had someone put that parcel in my valise while I was on the train to Calais—and then retrieved it in Calais while I was in the north helping with the wounded? But why?

If the police had come through the train searching the luggage, perhaps that Highland painting would have aroused little suspicion in the hands of a Scotswoman. And then there were the flecks of paint. That ugly painting . . . had it been hastily overlaid on some more recognizable work? If not properly dried, it would flake. Had whatever was underneath it been looted from a house or museum in Belgium or northern France?

I had no proof.

There was nothing I could do without it. Those flecks of paint and that string would be gone by the time I'd even found a constable. It would be my word against the shop-keeper's.

Turning down the Highland scenes I'd been shown, I wandered around the shop for a few minutes, as if still in search of something my father would like. In fact, I was looking to see if there was anything out of place here.

And I found it. A small study by Frans Hals. It was the same size and shape, certainly, as my parcel, and I couldn't imagine how such a treasure had come to be in such a small shop. I turned to ask the proprietor how much he was asking for the work, and he told me that it was already sold, hastily offering me another painting by a lesser-known artist.

I replied that I couldn't make up my mind what my father would like, and I promised to come back soon to see if there was something new on display.

"Money is no object," I said casually. "It's my father's happiness that matters."

He bowed me out of the shop, and I left knowing that the Frans Hals would disappear before I'd walked fifty feet.

What was I to do about this? What could I do?

The question, as it happened, was moot. That very day our orders were posted.

To my great disappointment, I was not sent to France straightaway. I expect it was because I was untested, and far from being fully trained. But I felt I was ready, and I chafed at the delay.

I was posted to Dover, to meet the boats coming in with wounded and help with the transfer to the trains for London. There, sorted and examined on the journey, men would be dispersed to whatever hospital or clinic was best suited to their wounds. Many of them were heavily drugged, to make the journey easier. Some were awake and screaming, while others lay in shocked or dazed silence, too badly injured to respond to our questions or our care. The doctors during our training had told us that the worst wounds, the appalling, mind-shattering ones, never left the battlefield. And yet despite my experience I had to learn all over again to ignore my own reaction to what I saw, and consider the needs of the patient.

I talked to those I could, sometimes asking after Rory and Bruce without mentioning that they were cousins, hungry for fresh news. Cousin Kenneth had written to say that Bruce was now listed as missing and there had been no further word of him since that time. Rory had not been heard from either, but then his name had not appeared on any of the lists. And that I had to accept as accurate.

If Rory was alive when I left France, then I prayed he was still alive.

But Cousin Kenneth's letter had taken so long to reach me, having been sent first to Cornwall, then forwarded to Mrs. Hennessey's, that anything could have happened since it was written.

And then one morning as I was walking down the hill toward the quay Sister Tomlinson came running after me, calling, "Sister? There's a letter for you."

I turned and saw that she was all smiles as she waved the envelope. "It came with the morning post, and I just discovered it. From France. From the look of it, it traveled by way of China."

Good news, I prayed. Let it be good news. Of Alain,

or Madeleine and Henri. Waiting for her to catch me up, I stood there in the autumn sunlight with the sea breeze on my face, my mind running ahead.

But then I saw it was an English envelope, forwarded many times. To the closed London house, to Scotland, to Cornwall, to Mrs. Hennessey, and now here in Dover where we were quartered. The postal service, with its usual fervor, had tracked me down, war or no war.

I didn't recognize the handwriting. I'd never seen it before. Not Rory, then, nor anyone else in the family.

I turned it over and broke the seal, slipped out the single sheet inside and unfolded it.

No one could tell me what had happened to you. The ambulance was not there, having gone north again, and no one had seen a young woman walking about alone, no one had been given a message for me. For God's sake, let me know if you are all right.

It was signed, simply, *Peter.*

And below, he'd written his Expeditionary Force address.

I stood there staring at the message.

He had known about the London house, he'd tried to find me there, unaware that it was shut for the duration.

I looked at the date. The end of September. He'd been alive then. He must be frantic—

I said, "I must answer this. Straightaway. Will you cover for me? For just an hour?"

Sister Tomlinson, amused, said, "Is he so important then? I declare, you went white as a sheet as you read the letter. You didn't tell me you had a beau."

I hadn't told her—or anyone else—that I was promised. The Service was not keen on young women with marriage on their minds. We were trained to serve and heal, not to dream. I'd thought it best to say nothing.

"He's not a beau. A friend."

She gave me a look that told me how well she believed that lie, then said, "Go on, write your letter. You'd do as much for me."

I thanked her and rushed back to our quarters, breathless from running up the hill. Pulling my letter box from under the bed, I took out an envelope, sheets of paper, a pen.

And then sat there, staring at them, tongue-tied.

What to say to him? How should I address him? Would he even get this letter I couldn't write?

Calm down, I told myself. Answer his questions. He's worried, just tell him you're all right.

I began, *Dear Captain Gilchrist,* the proper salutation of a letter to a man I knew slightly. But our acquaintance was more than slight . . .

I balled up the sheet and threw it across the room.

Peter.

> *Your officious Major discovered me, put me in his staff car under guard—well, the driver's stern eye—and sent me off to Rouen to find a ship for England. I did, arrived safely in Portsmouth, and since then I have finished*

*my training as a nursing Sister. I did leave a message of
gratitude with the Lieutenant accompanying the Major,
but I suppose no one thought to pass it along. You can
reach me at the address below, because the London house
is shut and I have taken lodgings to simplify my living
arrangements. Hotels are overflowing here, as well as in
Calais. Please, stay safe.*

Elspeth

I reread it twice, nearly balled it up as well, and then
sat there staring at it. The last sentence said so little when
I wanted to say so much. Had it been too forward to give
him Mrs. Hennessey's address? Did it suggest that I wanted
to hear from him? Or was it simple courtesy, telling him
where to find me?

Adding *Letters are regularly forwarded to wherever I
happen to be,* I folded the sheet, put it in its envelope, wrote
Peter's name and direction on it, and then searched for a
stamp.

More time had passed than I realized. Leaving Peter's letter in my box, I took my own with me, threw the
balled-up sheet into a dustbin after tearing it to shreds—
Sister Tomlinson was sweet but overly curious—and then
went off down the hill again.

I found an officer I knew who agreed to put it in the official post bag, and then I went to take up my duties.

Sister Tomlinson said, "I should have thought you'd be
away all morning, answering."

"No," I said, smiling sweetly. "I couldn't think of a thing to say."

Curiosity writ large in her eyes, she said, "It was addressed to Lady Elspeth Douglas. I happened to notice."

I felt cold. Summoning my wits, I replied, "I knew the Captain when we were children. He's always called me that. She was a Scots heroine, and he teased me because I was probably named for her."

"Was she in one of Sir Walter Scott's books?"

"It was an old story my mother used to read to us," I said, grateful that she hadn't seen my cousin Kenneth's letter on the stationery with the embossed coronet at the top.

A week later as I was checking the identity cards on the more seriously wounded, I saw a head of red hair covered with a very bloody bandage and felt the shock of instant recognition. It was Rory, and I went quickly to him, looked at his card, and then said, "Can you hear me? It's Elspeth, my dear. You're home. In England."

He opened his eyes. They were dazed with pain, but with a head wound, there was no relief that could be offered.

"Elspeth?" He frowned, trying to see my face clearly. "Is it you?"

"Yes, of course it is," I said, smiling. I could see how a bullet had scraped his skull, the skin raw where the bandage ended. "Would you like some water?"

"Why are you dressed like that?" he asked. "Is there a

costume party?" And after a moment he added, "My father did write, didn't he? I'd forgot." He fought the confusion, and then his mind cleared. "Yes, I'm very thirsty."

I held him so that he could drink, and he said as he finished sipping the cool water, "You shouldn't be doing this sort of work."

"I'm good at it. I want to do it," I told him. "Please, Rory, don't tell your father. It's important to me."

"All right. I won't give you away."

"Is there any word of Bruce?"

"Yes, thank God. He was a prisoner, but managed to escape."

I felt a guilty rush of relief. So far our family had fared better than most. So many hadn't been as lucky.

And then I was called away. When I came back, Rory had been put on the train and there was no time to go and search for him.

I wanted to write to my cousin Kenneth that night, to tell him that Rory had been wounded but that I believed he wasn't in any danger. But how could I, without explaining where I'd come by such information? I was supposed to be in Cornwall, not in Dover. The Army would inform him soon enough, surely.

I fought a battle with my conscience over my decision.

In the end, I asked Sister Tomlinson to write the letter. Curious, she wanted to know why I couldn't attend to it myself.

"After all, you saw this officer. You judged his condition."

I hadn't realized that my decision to become a nursing

Sister would be so fraught with peril. I was becoming quite adept at lying.

"I know his brother," I said finally. "I shouldn't care to have the family think my letter was an attempt to curry favor."

She laughed. "An Earl's son? You're remarkably foolish, Elspeth. How could you not wish to have them in your debt?" But she wrote the letter as I dictated it, and I was grateful.

There was always the possibility that with his multitude of contacts in the War Office, the Home Office, and the Foreign Office my cousin would hear that his ward was in the Nursing Service. And if he didn't approve, he could easily put an end to it. What I hoped was that by the time he discovered the truth, I'd have had a chance to demonstrate my skill, to prove that I was a good nurse, something to weigh in the balance against his disapproval. A very small hope, but all I had.

The opportunity that I'd been waiting for came sooner than expected. With only twenty-four hours' warning, seven of us were ordered to France to relieve Sisters who were being rotated home with the next convoy. I sent word to Mrs. Hennessey to hold my letters until I knew where I'd be posted and boarded the next ship to make the crossing to Calais.

• *Chapter Five* •

THE FIRST PERSON I SAW as we made our way out of Calais toward the Front was Henri Villard, arguing with a British officer in the middle of the road.

Our ambulance driver was on the point of sounding his horn when I put a hand on his arm, then jumped out my door to speak to Henri. He was wearing a Major's uniform; he'd been promoted. Except for new lines in his face, he appeared to be healthy, no signs of wounds, no limp, no stiff arm . . .

As I approached he was just turning away from the British officer, his face like a thundercloud. I don't think he even recognized me when I spoke his name—his mind was still on the argument he'd apparently lost.

"Henri? It's Elspeth—Elspeth Douglas."

He stared at me blankly, then took in my uniform, his gaze finally coming to rest on my face.

"Dear God!" was all he could manage. "What are you doing here?"

"Henri, have you heard from Madeleine? Do you know

you have a son?" I asked quickly, for my driver would be impatient to be on his way.

"Yes, her letter found me three weeks after he was born. I was frantic with worry. I wrote to her in return, but the mails are chaotic. She wants me to come to Paris, to see the boy, but how can I?" He gestured around us at the lorries and the wounded, the columns of troops and the long lines of ambulances heading the other way. "I'm here as temporary liaison with the British, but I might as well be in Corsica, for all the good it does me."

"I'm sorry," I said, "I know it must chafe. But I don't think our side knows what's happening either. It's all been so quick. Henri, is there word of Alain?"

"You haven't heard? He's missing. Somewhere in the Marne. There is hope that he was taken prisoner, but so far we've learned nothing to substantiate that."

My heart turned over, and I could feel Alain's ring against my skin. It seemed almost too heavy to bear. Like Henri's news.

"Missing? But surely—"

Henri shook his head. "You've no idea what it was like in those first weeks."

"I saw the Paris taxis set out for the Front. I was there."

"Were you?" He seemed to find that hard to take in. "You were still in France?"

Behind me, the ambulance driver hit the horn, and both of us jumped.

"Yes, Madeleine went into labor that very day. I must go."

He reached out, took my arm. "Elspeth, thank you for all you did for Madeleine. For the child. I won't forget. My family owes you more than I can ever repay."

He leaned forward, kissed me on the cheek, and then said, "Be careful. Please."

"And you."

Then he was gone, and I was clambering back into the ambulance. Before I had the door closed, we were lurching forward, catching up with the line of lorries and other ambulances heading toward the fighting.

I sat back in my seat, thinking of Henri and Madeleine. Of Alain.

Missing? That could mean he was a prisoner, or that his body had never been found. Even that he was badly wounded and no one at the French hospital knew who he was. There was no way of guessing which, and if the French Army couldn't find him, how then could I?

We were out of Calais now, on what passed for a road that was so deeply rutted and scarred it was impossible to make any speed at all. The signs of devastation were all around us soon enough, shelled villages, blasted orchards, toppled church towers, ruined convents, a land of the dead. Horses littered the verges, and cows, all dead, and there were rough crosses here and there where people too had died.

Familiar to me from my earlier experience, but to the other nurses it seemed like a moonscape, with nothing about it to show what once had been here. I could hear them, in the back of our ambulance, exclaiming in horror.

We were passing a column of Scots troops, and I scanned them for faces I knew. And then I saw him, at the head of the column, in deep conversation with another officer.

"Peter? Peter, it's Elspeth," I cried out the window.

He heard my voice, turned to look, and then we were past him, moving steadily forward. Out of reach, out of touch.

But leaning out my window, I saw him lift a hand in greeting.

I settled back into my seat once more, smiling. My driver said, "Do ye know half the Army, then?"

I didn't answer. My heart was still thundering in my chest, and I could hardly believe my luck. *I'd seen Peter.* He was alive, he was well. First the letter, and now this, however brief an encounter it was.

And then the euphoria seeped away. He was marching toward the fighting, not away from it. Today— tomorrow—he would be in another battle. I could find him in my aid station, bloody and half recognizable. Or lying there on a stretcher, already dead.

But even that would be better than his being taken to another station. Where I would never know if he lived or died of his wounds.

Uncertainty was as unsettling as knowing, but then war carried no guarantees in its wake.

It was nightfall when we reached our post. In the darkness ahead we could see the flashes of artillery salvos, feel the earth shake as the shells exploded. But there was no time to dwell on that. A row of stretchers waited for us, orderlies moving amongst them, and then we were taking our places beside the handful of Sisters already at work. The doctor had been killed two days before, and we found ourselves doing what we could to save men who needed care beyond our skills.

I spent the next week working feverishly to keep men alive, to prevent infection setting in and taking away a life that shouldn't have been lost. For infection was the enemy we all faced, doctors, nurses, patients. A bit of cloth, a bit of earth, anything driven into a wound, too tiny for the eye to see, could make the difference in survival. I reached a point where I hardly looked at faces, only at shattered bodies, and prayed while I worked that this one or that one would live against all odds. Thank God another doctor was quickly sent up to us, and when he slept I couldn't have told anyone. I myself was short of sleep, we all were. And then there was a lull in the fighting, and we finally caught up. I stood there, hands on my back, stretching weary muscles as the last of the patients left for hospitals behind the lines.

"Go to bed," Sister Maynard told me. "Sleep while you can."

"You're as weary as I am," I answered.

"I slept a little, earlier. Go on."

I thanked her and was on my way to my quarters when a shadow stepped out of the deeper patches of darkness by the tents.

Startled, I opened my mouth to call out to Sister Maynard when the shadow's torch flicked on and I saw that it was Peter Gilchrist.

"Oh, you gave me such a fright," I exclaimed as he turned off the torch. "I couldn't imagine—"

"I shouldn't be here," he said quietly. "But I kept looking for you. Earlier, on the Ypres road. I couldn't understand what had happened. Whether you were safe, or something had gone wrong."

"But you must have got my letter."

"Have you written? We've been on the move, and the post hasn't caught up. When first I saw you there on the road last week I thought you had never left France. And then I recognized the uniform. I knew then that you must have reached London safely."

I told him what had happened that day, and he nodded. "The Major. He's been relieved, thank God."

I couldn't invite him into my quarters, and there was nowhere else that was even remotely private where we could talk. But before I could say anything, he took my arm and was leading me toward a battered motorcar.

"It's Lieutenant Harding's motor. He bought it from a Captain who was shot outside Mons. I don't know who owned it before that. It has quite a history, apparently."

Surprisingly the seats were intact, and he held the door for me, then walked around to sit behind the wheel.

"I didn't know you were a Sister," he said.

"I wasn't. Not when we met on the Ypres road. When I got back to England, it seemed to be a very sensible thing to do."

"I can't imagine your cousin agreeing to this."

"He has no idea."

Peter chuckled.

"I don't believe anyone knew who I really was, when I went into training. I was Elspeth Douglas of Cornwall. A nobody whose late father was a Scot. I now live in a flat with three other nursing Sisters, or possibly there are four now. It's not even half the size of the small drawing room in the castle. I sleep in a room that the lowliest drudge in the kitchen would distain. But then I hardly had time to sleep, the training was so rigorous."

"You are remarkable," he said. I could see his smile, a flash of white teeth in the darkness. "But I must tell you that it's far too dangerous to work in forward aid stations. I wish you would ask for a transfer to a rear hospital."

Astonished, I could only stare at him. Finally I said, "I thought you of all people would understand. That day on the road to Ypres—it changed me. I don't think about the danger, only about broken bodies, men dying."

He was silent for a time and then he said, his voice different in the darkness, "That day changed me as well. I think I'm in love with you, Elspeth Douglas. And I can't protect you, if you walk into danger."

My mind was in a whirl. He shouldn't be telling me such things. There was Alain, there was the ring—

And there was Peter, sitting so close to me I could feel the warmth of his body in the cramped confines of the motorcar. I could remember his arm around me in the ambulance, the way his dark eyes crinkled at the corners when he smiled.

Alain was quite possibly the handsomest man I knew.

Peter was black Scots, tall, dark, and not handsome at all in the conventional sense. And yet there was something about him, something I couldn't name, but it was compelling, and it drew me. It was his face I saw in my dreams. The guilt of that was suddenly more than I could bear.

"For God's sake, say something," he said as the silence dragged on.

"Peter, please—"

And then a torch flashed across our faces, and I saw the outline of Dr. Colton behind it.

"What's going on? I thought I heard a motor coming up."

"Dr. Colton. This is Captain Gilchrist. He's a friend of the family. He's in the line not far from here and he came to see if I was all right."

Peter got out and extended his hand to Dr. Colton, who after the briefest hesitation, took it.

"I'm sorry if I've caused a bother," he said easily. "I encountered Sister Douglas on the way to her quarters, and we've been sitting here talking."

"She should be sleeping," Dr. Colton replied, casting a glance at me. I wondered if my guilt was writ large on my face, and if he read into it more than he should.

"Yes, I know. I was just leaving."

I got out of the motorcar, realizing that Dr. Colton expected it of me.

"Good night, then," Dr. Colton said, and with a nod, he walked away, giving us a final moment of privacy.

The width of the motorcar separated us, Peter and me.

I said, "Peter. It's too soon." It was all I could find to say. This was not the time nor the place to explain Alain. Not after Dr. Colton's interruption. And I wasn't sure what I wanted to tell him. I couldn't be falling in love with him. I couldn't—

"Yes, I know. I ought not to have spoken. But war makes a mockery of propriety sometimes. There's no way I could speak to your cousin, now or in the foreseeable future. Will Rory do? He's somewhere here in France."

"He's just been taken back to England with head wounds," I said.

"Ah." There was desolation in that one word. Peter looked toward the Front, his dark brows drawn together in a frown. "Still, I can't say that I regret telling you. There are no guarantees of tomorrow, are there? And it's probably better if we wait for peace and know where we stand. But I'm yours, yours to command. I want you to know that. Whatever happens."

And then he was getting back into the motorcar.

I couldn't very well say, *Thank you for coming* . . . I couldn't very well walk around to the driver's door, closer to him. All my training in the proper way to address everyone from the bootblack to the Queen, and I was at a loss when it really mattered.

Peter tried to make it easier for me. He smiled, that flash of white teeth, and I could imagine it touching his eyes as he said gently, "My dear girl, I've everything to live for now. You haven't seen the last of me."

I smiled. And then realizing that in spite of his boast,

I might never see him again, realizing how easily life was snuffed out by a bullet, a bit of shrapnel, the finality of a shell landing in the wrong place, I quickly moved forward, reached through the open window into the motorcar, and offered him my hand.

I hadn't thought—clutching the windowframe with my right hand, I'd given Peter my left—and there was no ring upon it now. But he wasn't to know why. He took it, held it for a moment, his fingers warm as they enclosed mine, then he lifted it to his lips, turned it over, palm up, and kissed it.

As I stepped back, he reversed, and then he was swallowed up by the darkness, the sound of the motor fading in the distance.

I walked on to my quarters, still feeling the touch of his lips on the palm of my hand, wondering how in the name of God I was to sleep after Peter's visit.

The cold reality of life intruded as I lay down on my cot. Alain was missing. Possibly killed in action. Under the circumstances, I had no right to listen to Peter's promises or anyone else's.

I was committed to Alain. Until such time that I could in honor tell him that I loved someone else.

The question was, did I?

What were my true feelings for Peter Gilchrist?

Over the next few days it was a question that haunted me as we worked with the wounded, and it was all I could do to concentrate on the task at hand. Then Dr. Colton accused me of woolgathering as we dealt with a chest wound, and I made a concerted effort to put Peter Gilchrist out of my mind.

• *Chapter Six* •

WE WERE PUSHED BACK BY another German attack, scrambling to move ourselves and our wounded out of harm's way. I was in the last ambulance, my companions the dead. Their pale faces reflected the light from the shelling, and I thought, *They are the lucky ones, beyond pain and worry and grief.*

A letter from Madeleine, by some miracle, had reached me the day before. She wrote,

> *Henri saw you in France, much to his consternation. He had believed you were safe in England. My dear, how did this come about? You never mentioned it to me. How can you bear to work with the wounded? I am told that the sight of such terrible wounds can drive one mad. You must be a far braver soul than I. But what should I tell Alain if we are able to reach him finally? He will be so worried for you. The hope now is that he is prisoner of the Germans. He and his men were fighting a rearguard*

action to allow the main body of troops to move to a stronger position when he was cut off. He got most of those in his command clear of the encircling Germans, he and one sergeant holding them at bay, before he was overrun. It's believed that he was wounded, although no one was able to say how severely. We pray that it was not serious and that he has been able to survive in the wretched conditions of a prison camp. He has earned a medal for such courage. Meanwhile, young Henri is thriving. He has his father's blue eyes and my chin. When I think how much we owe you, I'm at a loss for words.

I read the letter again. Alain. Wounded? A prisoner? There was room to hope.

Missing so often meant *dead,* the body unrecovered. Unrecoverable.

But if he was a prisoner, wounded or not, he was no longer fighting. If the wound healed, he would live to see the end of the war. Safely out of it.

Knowing Alain, how that would chafe, it was hard to think of him in such straits. And how good was German medical care in a prison camp? I touched the ring at my throat, a talisman now for his safe return.

I'd tucked the letter away in my traveling box, the little portable desk that Bruce, my cousin, had given me when I first went to France to study.

To remind you to write, he'd said as I opened it.

He too had been a German prisoner. And he'd escaped. But at what cost?

There had been no news of Rory or Bruce since I left England, and I couldn't write to my cousin, not without giving myself away, the envelope itself betraying where I was, and why.

We beat our hasty retreat, set up the aid station again as soon as we safely could, and watched the long line of wounded come in. The machine-gun cases were the worst, I thought, although the burned pilot was nearly as bad. Watching those flimsy aircraft high above our lines was incredible, and I found myself wondering what it would be like to fly. My father had told me once that it was the last freedom.

New orders arrived, coming in with the next convoy of ambulances. I was reassigned to transfer duty. I was to accompany severely wounded men on their way to England for more care.

I went to Dr. Philips straightaway.

"I don't want to leave France," I said, showing him my orders.

He looked at them, then said, "You're a very good surgical nurse, Sister Douglas. I shall hate to lose you. But I can't change your orders. And it's important for you to have this respite. Leave will bring you back to us all the more rested and better able to serve these men."

It was meant for encouragement, but I didn't need respite. I had found on my arrival in France that all I'd learned in my training was just a beginning, that standing beside a doctor working on the worst cases had taught me more in a few minutes than I'd learned in days of working in the hospital in London. I could second-guess the doctor, put into his hands the scalpels and the swabs and the threaded needles and the scissors before he asked for them. The result had been so very uplifting, an indication of my ability to make a difference.

My flatmate, Bess Crawford, had written to me before I left London for Dover that she had discovered depths in herself that she hadn't been aware of, before she went to France.

> *It was amazing, and the most rewarding experience of my life. I could concentrate in the most appalling situations, I could remember what I had seen done and apply that knowledge myself when it was necessary. Do we all feel this way? I don't know. I shall have to wait and ask Mary and Diana if this was true for them as well.*

Well, I could tell her that it was true in my case. And I didn't want to lose those skills, that sharpness.

But three days later I was heading south, meeting a convoy just north of Calais, and relieving one of the Sisters who had brought it that far.

We had a train, and the wounded could be made more comfortable, the Sisters could watch over them far better than in an ambulance hurtling across the bleak and devastated countryside. I moved through the two carriages that I'd been assigned to cover, watching over my patients, seeing that they were kept hydrated and that any bleeding was discovered before it became dangerous.

And all the while I thought about Dr. Philips and the others in that forward aid station. Wishing I stood beside them, or was sorting the stretchers as they came in, or was looking in on our surgical cases to be certain they were stable.

I tried not to remember that Peter was fighting nearby.

The crossing was stormy, and the patients we'd transferred to the ship were often seasick. I cleaned up vomit and urine and never had time to ask myself if I felt queasy.

In Dover, the first person I saw as we were moving our stretchers to the waiting train was Diana. She hailed me from one of the carriages, came running, and enclosed me in a fierce embrace.

I hugged her in return with the same sense of relief. I'd grown quite fond of my flatmates, and I couldn't imagine now having gone off to Cornwall and never meeting them.

"You're all right, then. Mrs. Hennessey had had no news. We were worried."

"We were on the move, as often as not. The Front is shifting almost daily."

"I must see to my charges. Shall we have dinner in London?"

"I'd like that," I told her.

And off she went as I returned to my own duties.

We'd lost seven patients on the ship and another three on the way to London. Infection, fast moving, unstoppable. I had held four of them as they died and had wept for them, so close to home, so close to those they'd left behind.

It was almost a relief in London to turn my own charges over to the next contingent of Sisters and watch the train pull out for Hampshire, Wiltshire, and Sussex, where there were now hospitals in what had once been stately homes. Even manor houses had taken in their share of ambulatory wounded, for the London hospitals couldn't possibly have accommodated so many.

Diana and I walked to Mrs. Hennessey's house from the omnibus stop closest to her street. The late autumn air was surprisingly cold, and the London damp was penetrating. I'd forgot that, in northern France.

Diana, shivering beside me, said, "I've heard from Mary and Bess. Barely a letter, but enough to tell me they're well."

"I've heard very little. From anyone."

We opened the outer door to Mrs. Hennessey's house and stepped into the hall out of the wind. Mrs. Hennessey herself came hurrying from her flat to greet us, and I felt I'd come home.

"I've a bit of chicken," she said, after we'd exchanged news. "I'll put it on and we'll have dinner. Food is getting more and more scarce. You'll be glad of a good meal to-night, without having to go out again."

When, an hour later, Diana and I came down again, Mrs. Hennessey had set the table, cooked the chicken in an herb broth, and baked potatoes, carrots, and parsnips in the oven. Bustling about her kitchen humming to herself, she was glad to have company for the evening.

Pausing while the tea was steeping in the pot, she went to the desk in her sitting room and brought back a letter.

"This was well traveled," she said, handing it to me. "I didn't want to risk sending it on."

The envelope was stained, torn in places, my name and my direction in Cornwall nearly illegible. It was a miracle that it had reached there, much less survived to find me at Mrs. Hennessey's in London.

I recognized Alain's handwriting at once. And my heart was in my throat as I opened the envelope.

"Take it into the sitting room to read it, love," Mrs. Hennessey said gently. "In private."

And so I did.

It was written on the eve of battle, although not the one where he'd been captured, I thought. An earlier one.

My dearest Elspeth, I hope you are safely in England and out of danger. We've saved Paris, somehow, but it was a near-run thing, let me tell you. The Germans got much too far down the Marne, well past Villard. I hesitate to think what the house must have suffered at their hands. Henri will be devastated. The Germans are very determined, and we shall find it very difficult convincing them to return to their own country. The war that was to end by Christmas will be lucky to end in the new year. The worst of it is that I have no expectation of speaking to your cousin before the Spring. Now I must close and see this into the pouch. You are my anchor in this nightmare, and I consider myself a very lucky man. I think of you in Cornwall, well out of this, and it gives me peace.

But I wasn't in Cornwall.

"Good news?" Diana asked, coming into the sitting room.

I took a deep breath. "A dear friend, writing to say he's all right. Only it's been a long time since this was written. Latest word is that he could be a prisoner."

"I'm so sorry," she said, putting her arm around my shoulders. "Come to dinner and think about it later. There's nothing you can do tonight."

True.

I said as we went into the small dining room and took our places at Mrs. Hennessey's table, "Did you find it hard to convince people that you were right to become a nursing Sister?"

Diana rolled her eyes. "My parents. My brother. My friends. But I think they're slowly coming to realize that I'm doing my part in this war. My great-aunt told me that no decent man would want to marry me now. Mrs. Hennessey can tell her that that's not true."

As she passed the roasted vegetables, Mrs. Hennessey nodded. "Someone proposes at least once a week. Cheeky, if you ask me!"

We laughed. Such proposals were a part of our days, most of them made as the sedative took effect and their pain subsided or as a frightened soldier, hardly more than a boy, dealt with severe wounds.

"Is there no one you care for particularly?" I asked Diana.

"Well, there's Simon Brandon. He's a family connection of Bess's, and the most attractive man I've ever met."

Mrs. Hennessey tut-tutted. "Pay no attention to her. He's the nicest young man, and he would never flirt with the likes of our Diana. She's broken more hearts than the Army can mend." But it was clear to me that Diana was one of Mrs. Hennessey's favorites, for there was no censure in her tone of voice.

"I wonder sometimes if I'll ever truly fall in love. I like this person for his sense of humor, that one for his kindness, or another one for his cleverness," Diana said pensively. "Finding every quality that matters to me in one man? Is it possible?"

Mrs. Hennessey said, "I had no doubts when Mr. Hennessey came along. I can tell you that. And he made me very happy. I wasn't to know then, was I, how few years we'd have together. But I'll never regret marrying him."

Diana turned to me. "Have you found anyone in particular that you care about?"

I could feel myself flushing.

"Oh, do tell!" Diana said at once. "Is he anyone we know?"

I tried to adopt the same light tone. "He's the brother of a school friend. I was madly in love with him when I was thirteen. Sadly, he's much older and he hardly knew I existed. He told me so himself."

They laughed, as I'd meant for them to, and commiserated with me on my misfortune in love. I couldn't tell them that he was the one who was missing, possibly a prisoner. I hadn't quite learned to show my feelings as easily as Diana could, or even Mary. Lady Elspeth was always expected To Set a Good Example. Sister Elspeth had yet to lose that aspect of her upbringing in an Earl's household.

Still it was a cheerful meal, and I found myself enjoying it. The very ordinariness of it drew me into this circle of friendship. All of my flatmates were of good breeding, and I was very glad I could appear to be one of them, rather than set apart by an accident of birth. I'd grown up with a personal maid to dress me and a footman to run my errands, a coachman to take me wherever I wished to go, before my father replaced him with a motorcar and a chauffeur. My meals were served to me, rather than dishes passed around the table for each person to help him- or herself. I was accustomed to dressing for dinner and having wine with each course.

Did I miss all that? I was beginning to think that it belonged to another world, one I had shared with my father. Without him, I wasn't sure I wished to return to it.

I was glad to go up to our flat and prepare for bed. Diana and I were very tired, and we didn't linger over our tea. Mrs. Hennessey wished us a good night, and as Diana and I climbed the stairs, Diana said, "I wonder sometimes if I'll look back on this war as one of the happiest—and the saddest—periods of my life."

I knew what she meant. In spite of the fatigue, the heartbreaks, the nightmares, doing something that mattered had become more important to me with every passing day.

I was grateful after all for this respite in England. But I longed to be back in France.

And soon enough, I was.

Growing up I had known the names of all the proper regiments—the Scots Greys, the Guards, the Argyle and Sutherland, the Household Cavalry, the Buffs, and so on. But the lines were becoming blurred as they were depleted and new recruits were brought in to replace officers and men who had been wounded or killed. In place of old family names were those from small towns across England, Scotland, and Wales. A very different Army, but one none the less that fought bravely and did its best to hold the line against the Germans. But as the line wavered, so did our casualties increase.

Day after day we worked to keep as many alive as possible. For two weeks, Bess Crawford was posted to my sector, and we worked together as a team, side by side almost without talking, each of us instinctively knowing what the other required.

And then she was transferred to a new station, where her skills were badly needed. Not twenty-four hours later, we were moved back, before the morning's assault across No Man's Land.

I'd never traveled with so little before this, except when I left France in such a hurry. My kit consisted of essentials, pared down to uniforms and washing powder for them, a comb and brush, face powder, a toothbrush and tooth powder, and a second pair of sturdy shoes, a rain cape, and my nail case, to keep them short and clean. My one luxury was my letter box.

Even as a young girl, my trunks were packed for me by my maid, and included dinner dresses, riding clothes, suitable daytime dresses for making calls, gowns for evening parties or going to the opera, country walking clothes, and a proper dark dress for Sunday services or sudden deaths. With them went slips and camisoles, stockings and other undergarments. Added to that were hats and gloves, shoes and jewelry, the latter carried by my maid. My father generally took me everywhere he went, and I was expected to be turned out in style. The trunks and hatboxes and valises were sent to the railway station an hour before our own departure, and they arrived wherever we were going shortly after we crossed the threshold.

I had, I thought, learned to do without so many things, not just trunks of clothing. I wondered what my cousin Kenneth would have made of that. I wondered too how I was to return to that old life once the war was over.

Half an hour later, we'd reached our next destination only to be told that there was fierce fighting in the sector to our left, and we were held up, waiting for further news.

A trickle of wounded appeared out of the darkness, and we began to treat them, with orders to keep as quiet as possible. And then a stretcher party arrived at the run, and Sister Blake went forward to assess the severity of the wound. She called over her shoulder, "Sister Douglas—come quickly."

I did, to find a Highlander lying on the makeshift stretcher, a third man keeping pressure on a leg wound. It didn't take me long to see that an artery had been nicked by a piece of shrapnel, and I went to work quickly, speaking to the man in Gaelic, telling him that he would be all right. But I couldn't be sure. We put on a tourniquet, and after the worst of the bleeding stopped, I called for the doctor to decide whether we could operate to sew up the tear. My fear was the man had lost too much blood already, but even with the tourniquet I couldn't be certain there was no internal seepage that would kill him before we could do any more.

As the doctor walked over to us, one of the men with the wounded soldier said, "Ye must save him, he's the laird's foster brother."

I saw that the speaker was a piper—they often served as medical orderlies or stretcher bearers, brave men that they were.

"We'll do our best," I promised, and then the doctor was there, shaking his head as he examined the leg.

"It doesn't look good," he said to me under his breath. "Bind the wound tightly and pray that it clots sufficiently to save him."

I worked on, even when the order came to move at once, saying to the three Highlanders who had brought him in, "Keep watch. We dare not move him yet. The jolting could reopen that artery."

The others were calling to me to come at once, but I refused, staying with the wounded man and his attendants.

I understood what he represented. He was the laird's

foster brother, the clansman that the laird's parents chose to bring up with him, servant and companion and kinsman all in one. He was often the son of the wet nurse called in to care for the newborn heir, and the bond between these two was as strong if not stronger than a bond of blood. The clansmen who had brought him to us had been ordered by the laird, obviously an officer in their company, to take the foster brother to the nearest aid station, and although they were clearly worried about the rest of their comrades, their duty was never questioned.

We waited for over half an hour, the sounds of fighting coming closer all the time, and I could see the muzzle flashes of a machine gunner across the expanse of shell pits, blasted trees, barbed wire, and mud that lay between him and our own lines. And then the machine gun nest was knocked out, the assault turned in our favor, and the next thing we knew, the front line was surging forward, leaving us in a quiet eddy in its wake.

I examined the wound for the hundredth time, it seemed, and found that the bleeding had stopped. It was important to release the tourniquet at intervals, or the leg would be lost whether the bleeding stopped or not. And I had watched each time for signs that the tear in the artery was widening.

Finally I stood up, my legs aching from kneeling beside the stretcher on the rough earth, my apron and uniform covered in blood and mud and whatever else had been trampled into the soil as armies surged back and forth across it.

The Highlanders were on their feet as well. They had kept guard, rifles at the ready, during our long, anxious vigil, and they spoke to the wounded man now, their voices husky with relief.

We carried him back to where the aid station had been set up. After he had been seen to, his bandages changed and something given to him for the pain, his companions hurried back to the lines and their sector. I was summoned and dressed down for insubordination.

I listened meekly, letting the doctor's fear and anger wash over me. He'd have had a great deal of explaining to do if I'd been taken prisoner, even as lowly Sister Douglas, and yet he had had the safety of his entire station to think of. I had put him in a very difficult position, and I was aware of that.

Finally out of words, his anger draining away, he said, "And what do you have to say for yourself?"

"I have no excuse, sir. I thought only of the needs of the wounded man, and no one else. It was not well done on my part. But he's alive, and I can't help but feel that if I'd moved him—or left him to the ministrations of his companions—he wouldn't have been. They meant well, but they had no training."

"You have to remember, Sister, that we are here to save as many lives as possible, but that means on occasion we must make decisions about who will live and who will die. We cannot devote time needed by others to a hopeless case, however much we might wish to look for a miracle."

"I understand. I should not have put the entire aid station in jeopardy."

He made a frustrated noise, half a grunt, half a curse. "In truth, I should send you back to England to be disciplined. But you're a damned good nurse, young woman, and we need you. Do I have your word you will obey orders in future? Without question or delay?"

"I promise I will keep in mind that putting others at risk is wrong."

It was hardly my word given, but how could I promise when I didn't know what could happen in future?

Still, he was satisfied, and after a moment, considering me as if trying to read my mind, he nodded and walked back to the line of wounded.

Several hours later, I looked in on the foster brother, and I found him resting comfortably, very little seepage from the wound showing up on his bandages.

He was to be taken back to hospital with the next group, and I thought it was very likely now that he would live. I told him so in Gaelic, and he said, "Bless you, Sister."

Four days later, when there was a lull in the fighting, an officer came into the aid station searching for me.

I was just finishing bandaging a stomach wound. When that was done to my satisfaction, I walked out to find Rory Douglas standing there.

Throwing my arms around him, I held him close. I could still see the raw scar where his head wound had been, the way his hair had not yet grown back across the long groove that could just as easily have killed him.

"What are you doing back in France?" I demanded. "It's too soon."

"I heal quickly. Besides, my men needed me. I couldn't linger in England being cosseted while they were fighting and dying out here."

"Hardly cosseted," I replied.

I'd heard that same sentiment from dozens of officers, and I understood how Rory felt. But he wasn't just any officer, he was my cousin, and I couldn't imagine losing him to the Germans.

"You're experienced enough. You should be a staff officer now," I added, in a teasing tone.

He shook his head. "That's worse. No, I want to be where the fighting is."

With a sigh, I nodded. "That doesn't make it any easier for your family."

"Probably not," he said with that sheepish grin I remembered from our childhood. "I've news of Bruce. That's why I came. He's home. I don't think he'll see much more fighting. And he'll walk with a limp for the rest of his life."

The relief was overwhelming. While I loved all of my cousins almost like brothers, Bruce had always been my favorite. He reminded me so much of my father, in appearance and in small ways that were, after my father was killed, painful reminders. And yet even as my heart ached, watching him, I knew that I would always love Bruce for that familiar memory he could so easily evoke.

"I came here not only to tell you about Bruce, but to give you something. It seems that when Bruce was captured, he was taken with another contingent of British officers to a temporary camp where they were processed. It was there that he managed to escape. But before that, a convoy of French prisoners was brought in, and he discovered that one of them was Madeleine Villard's brother. Alain Montigny. Montigny gave him a message for you, in the event British prisoners were allowed to send and receive mail. He brought it home, and I've brought it to you." He considered me. "Bruce also said that Montigny told him that as soon as the war was over, he intended to speak to our father. Is there something between you, Elspeth?"

"A promise," I said. "He shouldn't have spoken, but he was leaving the next morning to join his regiment. He asked if I would give him permission to speak to Cousin Kenneth. I did."

"Yes, that's understandable. I'd have done much the same myself, in his shoes. But he'd been badly wounded, Elspeth. Whether he survived the move into Germany, I don't know."

"Madeleine told me he'd done something very brave."

"He had, and the Germans gave him no quarter as a result. A good man, my dear. I hope he comes home to you."

Rory put a scrap of paper into my hand, then said, "Stay safe, Elspeth. Bruce asked me to tell you that you're as mad as your father, but he loves you anyway."

I laughed, my fingers closing over the folded paper. "Go with God, Rory. I don't want to see you on our operating table. One wound is enough for glory."

He smiled, kissed me, and was gone, his tall figure striding toward the ambulance that had brought him this far. I waited until he was out of sight, then went to my quarters to read the letter from Alain.

My darling girl, I have no right to call you that, but in these straits, you will forgive me for thinking of you as my own. I have heard that Madeleine was safely delivered of a son, and that is good news. Your cousin will see that this reaches you somehow, to tell you that I am alive, have been wounded but not severely, thank God, and that my spirits lift with happiness whenever I think of you. If I come out of this whole, I shall look forward to making you my wife. Until then, my fondest love. Yours, Alain.

I felt hot tears fill my eyes, and with a twist of my heart that was part love, part guilt, I remembered our last night together in Paris. Alain entertained no doubts about that promise to me, and fool that I was, I could not say the same.

Why had I ever gone north on the Calais-to-Ypres road? Why had I not stayed in my hotel as I was told and waited until someone had come to arrange my crossing?

My stubborn headstrong nature. A belief that what I wanted to do was what I should do. Just like my father. And look what had become of him. Look at what I had promised Alain. How could I have felt anything for Peter Gilchrist if I were already heart and soul Alain's?

The ring hanging on its slender gold chain at my throat seemed to burn against my skin, a token not of love but of betrayal.

Did I love Alain? If I did, how could I be falling in love with Peter Gilchrist?

And what was I to do, with Alain a prisoner and wounded?

The next senior officer I saw, I asked if it was possible to get letters through to prisoners in German hands.

He could tell me how it was done with British prisoners. "Although I can guarantee nothing, you understand. It's not a perfect system."

But he had no idea how the French went about it.

• *Chapter Seven* •

As the fighting surged back and forth, and the warm autumn turned wet and colder, we worked long hours, nurses, orderlies, and doctors, to keep up with the constant flow of wounded.

One afternoon when there was a long line of stretchers waiting for treatment, I recognized one of the bearers. It was the piper I'd seen when I treated the foster brother.

He inclined his head, and I paused in my duties to speak to him.

"Did your laird's foster brother survive? There's been no word since he was taken away in the ambulance."

"Aye, Sister, he did. We're verra' grateful."

"I'm glad for his sake." I started to move on, when the piper stopped me.

"Ye have the Gaelic, Sister."

"I was brought up in the Highlands," I said, smiling.

"I would like to know your name."

"Douglas. Sister Douglas."

"A bonnie name for a bonnie lass," he said, with no intention of flirting. It was an acknowledgment of a common past.

I walked on. There were hundreds of Scots soldiers in France, wearing not their own tartans but that of their regiments. It was impossible to tell a Chisholm from a MacLeod or a MacGregor from a Campbell. For many of them it was a way out of poverty, and fighting was a tradition down the centuries. I'd grown up with tales of battles and feuds. Stirring tales, some of them, tales of treachery and vengeance many of them. The Borders had seen a no less bloody history, sometimes fighting the English, sometimes fighting each other.

My father had had his own piper, one of the finest in Scotland. He'd played "Flowers of the Forest" for my father's funeral, and piped him to his grave. I could still remember MacLachlan's tall, straight figure walking ahead of me, the pipes over his shoulder, his stride that of a soldier, and the music seeming to swirl over and around me, offering the only comfort I'd felt since the news had been brought to me. And that night, beneath my windows, the piper had played again, this time for me. For the last time.

The Earl is dead. Long live the Earl.

The next morning, Rob MacLachlan became my staid cousin Kenneth's piper, but he had had no heart for that. I never again heard him play as he had for my father. Indeed, six months later he was dead, and while the doctor reported it was age, I knew better. He had not wanted to live on without my father.

I sighed as I turned to my next patient. It was clear that this war was not ending anytime soon. It was devolving into the dreaded stalemate that sent wave after wave of brave men charging across No Man's Land, and bringing wave after wave of wounded and dying back to us.

I'd had no news of Rory since we'd spoken, and no news at all of Captain Gilchrist. I could have asked any of the Scots that passed through my hands if they knew of him, but I had resolved not to press the issue. The more time and distance between us, the better for my peace of mind. *And very likely for his as well,* I thought bleakly. Perhaps— perhaps he would forget me, given time.

I was asked to accompany another convoy of wounded to England, and once again I tried to persuade the doctor in charge to let me stay where I was. And once more I was told I needed to be relieved.

"You're tired, Sister Douglas. I see it in your face, the circles under your eyes."

But that wasn't because of my duties, I wanted to tell him—and couldn't. It was worry about something else, and that would never do. The Service was quite firm about divided loyalties.

I said, "You need to rest more than I do."

Dr. Tennant grinned. "I know. But who will step into my shoes?"

"Who will step into mine?" I retorted before I could stop myself.

"There's that," he agreed. "But Sister Blake is a fine nurse, and we'll manage, I'm sure. Now go and pack your kit. The ambulances will be coming forward in another hour."

And so it was that I found myself once more on my way to England.

Sister Blake put a slip of paper into my hand as I was leaving. "It was my mother's home in Sussex," she said. "If you don't have time to go to Scotland or Cornwall, this is a lovely place to spend a few days. You won't regret it."

"I shouldn't like to intrude on your family—a stranger," I responded, but she shook her head.

"No one has lived there for the past three years. Not, in fact, since my mother's death. It's a happy cottage, and I wouldn't mind knowing that it's being lived in again. Mrs. Wright, just across the road, will see to your comfort. Give her my love, if you go down."

I thanked her, shoved the slip into my pocket, and got into the last ambulance.

"Bring me a walnut," she called as we pulled out. "From the tree in the front garden." And I waved to her.

Shelling commenced again shortly after we set out, and I could picture the long lines of wounded coming in to the aid station this day. Shrapnel made such ghastly wounds, slicing into flesh and bone. There was no protection.

And then I had no time to think of anything else but the men in the back of my ambulance.

A wound reopened, and we had to stop while I bandaged it again. Another soldier, a sergeant, already in the throes of delirium from a high fever, thrashed and tossed, shouting incoherent orders to the men he'd left behind. I gave him a sedative and stayed with him until it took effect, swaying with the rough motion of the ambulance and holding on to one of the metal struts. I was glad to clamber again into the passenger seat when next we stopped to add another three cases to our own.

We rolled into Calais in the dead of night and were directed straight to the ship waiting to take wounded on board. We off-loaded our stretcher cases, including two that had died en route in spite of all that we could do, and I went to find the English officer in charge to have my papers stamped.

That dealt with, I hurried back to the ship, an orderly with me, and we found seven men in furious argument at the foot of the gangway.

There was a stretcher on the ground, a man in a torn, bloody uniform lying on it, his chest heavily bandaged. I marched up to the group and said, "What's the problem?"

"He's not on the list," one of the port sergeants informed me. "He was brought in by another convoy, and he's too ill to make the transit. Now the local hospital insists that he be taken to England if he's to have any chance at all. But no papers came with him. Or if they did, this lot"—he pointed to the stretcher bearers—"haven't got them."

I turned to the men who had brought the stretcher to the ship, and at once I recognized the piper.

"What's the trouble here?" I asked him in Gaelic.

"He willna' let the laird go aboard. And if he doesna', the laird could die."

For the first time I looked down at the pain-ridden face,

thin and heavily bearded, long dark lashes sweeping cheeks flushed with fever.

It was Peter Gilchrist.

It took me all of several seconds to school my expression. The last thing I must do, I told myself, is to appear to have a personal interest in this man's welfare. But I couldn't stop my fingers from touching his cheek.

"What nonsense," I said, straightening up to confront the harbor authorities. "This man should go aboard. That's a dangerous fever and must be treated quickly. He can't wait for the next ship. I take full responsibility for this decision." I turned to the piper and his companions. "Return to your company. I'll keep him safe."

The piper stood his ground. "I willna' leave him."

The Army did not recognize clan loyalties. The piper could be court-martialed for desertion. I said in Gaelic, "You must return to your company. Please, I will see to him. If you go with us, the Army will shoot you."

I could see that he was about to argue the matter.

"Tell me how to reach you. I will send word."

I handed him paper and a pencil, and he wrote down his regiment and company, his address in France. Reluctantly he passed it to me. I put it in my pocket with the paper that Sister Blake had given me, then said to the port officer, "These men will see him aboard and then leave. Or do you have stretcher bearers?"

"We don't," he said shortly, preparing to object. "This is highly irregular, Sister."

"Take it up with Lord Hamilton, if you doubt me. He

will tell you that you have made the right decision. This man is his cousin, and if he dies, Lord Hamilton will be very displeased."

I hadn't used that tone of voice in many weeks. It was Lady Elspeth's voice, and it brooked no argument. What's more, the sergeant knew who Lord Hamilton was.

After the briefest hesitation, he ordered the stretcher taken aboard, and the gangway was raised on the heels of the departing Scots.

We were at sea ten minutes later. I hastily put both the piper's direction and that of the Sussex cottage that Sister Blake had given me into my letter box and began my rounds. There was much to do and little time in which to do it, as the crossing didn't take very long.

I saw to my patients from the aid station, then made my report to Matron, who was in charge of the convoy crossing.

And finally I had a few minutes to look in on Peter Gilchrist. He had been taken to the ward for the severely injured, and the Sister in charge said, as I came to stand by his cot, "I have no paperwork for him."

"He was a last-minute addition, owing to his fever and an infected wound."

"Well, he most certainly has those." She smiled as she turned to me. "A very attractive man, isn't he? We'll do our best to see that he survives."

In the end, I helped her cut away the bandage over Peter Gilchrist's chest.

The wound was not shrapnel, thank God, but he had been shot through the upper chest, possibly clipping a lung, for his breathing was uneven. And there was probably some damage to the ribs or the shoulder. We had no X-ray machine to see for ourselves. The main problem was the fever, indicative of infection, and we cleaned the wound again, put septic powder on it, and then wrapped it in fresh bandages.

"I'll give him something to bring down the fever. Can you lend a hand in this ward, Sister Douglas? There are more criticals than usual, and the Sister assigned to me was still in surgery at the hospital in Calais when we sailed."

After making certain I could be spared from looking after my own patients, I stayed, helping in any way I could. Keeping an eye on Peter Gilchrist was not difficult. After all he was amongst those in my care, and as I made my rounds, I could stop and observe him, just as I did everyone else.

I hadn't realized how shaken I was by finding him in such straits. I was too good a nurse not to know that he could very likely—would more than likely—die from the infection raging through his body. Trying to imagine a world without Peter was beyond me, and I could only pray that I was there beside him if the unthinkable happened.

"Are you all right?" Sister Taylor asked me, casting a stern look in my direction after I'd dropped the tin of septic powder a second time.

"The sea. Perhaps I'm not the sailor I thought I was," I answered, and she nodded.

"It took me several crossings to get used to the Channel," she said sympathetically. "It is surprisingly rough today. But keep your mind on your patients and your stomach will stay down."

Several of them were seasick, agony for wounded men, and I held foreheads, brought cool cloths, and offered what comfort I could. There were orderlies to help, but even they were feeling the wild yawing and dipping of the ship. Carrying buckets of vomit up to the decks made their duties even worse.

Sister Taylor came up behind me as I stood watching Peter breathe. Was it a little more ragged than it had been? *Please God, let me be wrong,* I prayed.

She said, her voice kind, "You're worried about him, aren't you? Not just the infection. Do you know"—she glanced at his tag—"Captain Gilchrist?"

"I do know him. He lives not far from where I grew up in Scotland. He's a friend of one of my cousin's."

"How sad. That fever's not breaking. You should prepare yourself."

She hadn't meant to be pessimistic, she was only assessing his condition as a trained nursing Sister would. But her words were like knives in my heart.

We were five miles out of Dover when Peter opened his eyes for the first time.

I was there as his sight cleared. He recognized me, saying with a frown, "Elspeth? What are you doing here? There's heavy fighting, you must get out."

The confusion of delirium.

I said, "We're on a hospital ship. We'll be in Dover very soon. You've been wounded, Peter. Are you in pain? Thirsty?"

But he couldn't quite comprehend what I was saying.

Taking my right hand in his left, he said, "My dear girl," and then his eyes closed again.

When we landed in Dover there was so much bustle offloading the wounded that I lost track of Peter. There was my own contingent of wounded to account for and sort by condition as well as three cases that one of the doctors coming on board had questions about. By the time I'd settled them on the train, Peter had been moved.

He was not on the master list of wounded, although I'd reported his presence to Matron, and she had promised to add his name at the bottom. I wanted one of the doctors to look at him before he was transferred to London. But the ship's critical ward where the more serious cases had been was empty now. I searched the other wards for Sister Taylor, and she was nowhere to be found. Indeed ratings were already swabbing the floors.

I went back up on deck in time to see the last of the ambulatory wounded being helped into the train. I was certain one of the nurses was Sister Taylor and I raced toward her, finally drawing close enough to call to her.

She looked around for a moment, as if not certain where the summons had come from, and then she saw me as she was helping the last of the leg wounds into a carriage.

"Sister Douglas. Going on to London, are you? I envy you. I've to take the orthopedic cases to a clinic in Suffolk."

I did indeed have forty-eight hours of leave. And I was prepared to spend them searching for Peter Gilchrist if I had to.

"I'm looking for Captain Gilchrist. The chest wound.

The one added to the list at the last moment. Has he already been put on the train? Or is he remaining in Dover at present?"

"The dark attractive one? Yes, he had a turn for the worse while you were seeing to your cases. I put him in with several other chest wounds. The doctor in charge was concerned—his fever had spiked, and that's never a good sign."

It meant the infection was spreading. It could mean death was imminent.

I said, "I'd like to know where he's being taken. It's important—if he's that ill, his brother ought to be informed straightaway."

"Yes, that would be wise. He's already aboard. Number one fifty-six. The third carriage, I think."

I thanked her and turned to walk along the carriages toward the one I was after. The stationmaster called to me from his office. The train was gathering steam, but he was insistent, and I had no choice but to stop and listen to him. Apparently he thought I was seeing the wounded off, and he wanted to tell me that transportation was available down to the ship just about to embark for France. The train was now pulling out of the station. Turning my back on him, I ran after it, waving and calling, frantic for someone to open a carriage door for me so that I could swing myself aboard.

And the ambulatory wounded at the windows waved back and blew me kisses, believing, like the station master, I was only saying good-bye to someone.

I stopped at the edge of the platform, out of breath from running, feeling desperately tired, desperately afraid.

But there was nothing I could do.

I watched the train growing smaller in the distance as it climbed up from the port.

And then behind me, I heard a man swear.

I turned, just as he saw me and apologized.

"Sorry! I just missed that blasted—Lady Elspeth? Is that you? And in uniform? My God, I didn't know you were a nurse!"

It was Tommy Nesbitt, with whom I'd dined and danced and casually flirted any number of times, a dear friend who had gone to school with my cousin Rory.

He was wearing the uniform of a staff officer, a Major, and I said, "Yes, your eyes aren't deceiving you. I didn't know you'd gone back to your regiment."

He'd resigned his commission when his father died and taken over the family estates.

"Yes, there was nothing for it but to put on the uniform again. But what are you doing here in Dover?"

I explained about the convoy of wounded. "I was supposed to be on that train," I ended, "but the stationmaster stopped me, and it was gone before I could do anything."

"Well, I must be in London for a meeting tomorrow morning, but they held me up at the castle. I can't afford to wait. Come with me, and let's see what can be done."

I went with him, and we caught up on what had become of mutual acquaintances. I told him about Bruce—he hadn't heard the news—and about Rory, amongst others, and then said, "I just saw Peter Gilchrist as well—in fact, he's on that train, badly wounded."

"I'm sorry to hear that. Peter and I are good friends."

We were part of a small social circle, and it wasn't surprising that Tommy knew Peter.

We had reached the port commandant's office, and I waited in the anteroom while Tommy went in to speak to him.

He came out half an hour later, saying, "We're in luck! A Guards officer drove down to Dover on his way to France, and he's left his motorcar and his wife at one of the local hotels. She can't drive, and she's looking for someone to take her back to London."

We left the port and walked toward the line of hotels that faced the sea, popular before the war with travelers and holidaymakers. The Dover Strand was tall, white, and imposing, with turrets that—it was said—made it possible for one to see the coast of France on a clear day, given a good telescope. Indeed, brass ones were mounted on the narrow balcony that ran outside the long windows.

At Reception Tommy asked for Mrs. Larkin, and the hotel manager came out to speak with us. Apparently Mrs. Larkin had taken rooms for a fortnight but had changed her mind and was preparing to return to London, we were told. "She saw the ships bringing in the wounded, and it was too much for her. Recently married, you see."

I did see. She wouldn't care for any reminder that her husband too might be brought in on one of the hospital ships someday.

Tommy went up to speak to her, and when he came down he was carrying a valise. I suddenly realized that my kit was on the train I'd missed, in the baggage van with that of the other Sisters.

"The staff is seeing to the rest of her luggage," he said. "The motorcar is being brought around. Do you have a valise?"

"It will be in London before I am."

"Then we must set out as soon as Mrs. Larkin is ready."

She came down shortly after that, a tall thin woman whose eyes were red from crying.

Tommy presented me simply as Sister Douglas, and Mrs. Larkin frowned.

"I doubt there will be room for a passenger," she said crossly.

Tommy smiled. He wasn't a staff officer for nothing. His diplomatic skills were legendary. "I think we can manage quite well."

And indeed we did, under Tommy's direction. He regarded the motorcar for a moment, then instructed the hotel staff where to put Mrs. Larkin's small trunk and three valises. Grateful that she hadn't traveled with a maid as well, I tucked myself in a corner of the rear seat, a hatbox poking me in the ribs and a picnic basket taking up most of the room under my feet. I said nothing about that when Tommy asked if I were comfortable, for this was my only hope of reaching London before Peter was taken off that train.

Tommy was an excellent driver, threading his way through the busy port traffic, climbing past the castle, and settling down to a smart pace as we picked up the road to

London. Mrs. Larkin was quiet at first, and I wondered if she had begun to regret her decision to leave Dover. Very soon she began a querulous monologue, telling us about her fears for her husband, the shocking sight of so many wounded being brought in and the smoking ruins of a ship out in the Channel that had been torpedoed by a submarine.

"I quite understand that Raymond is a soldier," she said. "When I met him in Shropshire, there *was* no war. And even when Belgium was invaded, it all seemed so far away. And Raymond's regiment was on duty at Buckingham Palace. I had no idea it would be sent to France. Yes, all the young men I know were going on and on about getting into the thick of it. Rushing off to join the Army or the Navy. The Vicar's son went to be a flier, of all things. There should have been more than enough men to fight, and I can't think why Raymond was *needed*. He should have thought about *my* feelings, and stayed in London."

When she had married her soldier, it must have seemed an exciting life, lovely uniforms, regimental dinners, balls, their only worry being where they might be sent next, for most of the standing regiments took turn about postings to various parts of the Empire. Rory had served in South Africa, and he'd been on the point of going to Canada when Germany marched. Mrs. Larkin hadn't bargained on war and death. She wasn't prepared to cope with it.

Before we reached Canterbury, she had begun to cry, and it wasn't until Rochester that she breathed a huge sigh and said, "He'll be all right, won't he? I'm sure he will."

Tommy reassured her, and blessed silence fell at last. I'd have liked to talk to Tommy myself, but it would have been awkward from the rear seat, and Mrs. Larkin's presence prevented me from touching on anything personal.

We pulled into London late, and even though Mrs. Larkin was set on going directly to her brother-in-law's house, Tommy told her that I must meet a train at Victoria Station. With poor grace, she agreed, murmuring something about having to make the best of it. I wondered if Raymond was quite aware of the true nature of the woman he'd married.

The train was in the station when we arrived, and as I thanked Tommy and then Mrs. Larkin for bringing me to London, I could see a line of ambulances drawn up. Tommy walked with me to the gate, kissed me on the cheek, and told me to take good care of myself. And then he was gone.

The transfer of patients was already in progress, those intended for London hospitals or further treatment being carried on stretchers to the waiting ambulances, others being transported to other trains.

I walked down the line, looking for the third carriage, but it was already empty.

I found the Sister in charge, and she said, "Not now, please," as she dealt with the organized chaos. Impatient though I was, I admired her calm skill. Finally she turned to me. "Kits are in the baggage van, Sister."

"Yes. I'm looking for Captain Gilchrist. Chest wound, he was having difficulties when he was put into carriage three."

Her eyes narrowed as she studied me. "Is your interest professional or personal, Sister?"

"Professional. I was the sister who brought him on board, but I was occupied with paperwork in Dover when he took a turn for the worse. I'd like to know"—I had to fight to keep my voice steady—"to know if he survived the journey."

She nodded, consulting her list. "*D—E—F—G.* Ah. Gilchrist. Yes, his fever continued to rise. He was taken off in Rochester and sent to hospital there."

I stared at her. We had been in Rochester only hours ago. But I hadn't known—there was no way I could have known that Peter was there.

I thanked her, very quickly collected my kit from the baggage van guard, and then went to find the stationmaster.

But there was no seat on any train traveling to Dover. They were filled with troops, and the stationmaster said, "You'll have to show me orders, if you want to travel in that direction."

The only orders I had allowed me to travel back to Dover in three days' time.

"I have just a few hours of leave. I was hoping to see my family."

He couldn't be persuaded to give me space. And in England bribes were unacceptable.

In the end, I turned and walked out of Victoria, wondering how in the world I was going to reach Rochester. Tommy had already gone, and even if I could find him, he had an urgent meeting in the morning. This morning. Besides, the motorcar belonged to Mrs. Larkin. I didn't think she would allow me borrow it, under any circumstances. Not even if I used my title. A Scottish earldom carried little weight in Shropshire, I thought wryly.

A cab slowed as I stood undecided on the pavement.

"Sister?" he called, waiting to see if I wished a cab.

There was nothing more I could do. I nodded, just as he was about to give up and move on.

I got out at Mrs. Hennessey's house, and looked up at the windows belonging to our flat. No lights. It must mean that no one else was on leave at the moment.

I let myself in the door, climbed the stairs, and walked into the flat, feeling exhaustion overtake me.

As I hung up my coat on the rack by the door, a voice called drowsily from one of the other bedrooms.

"Mary? Diana? Elspeth?"

It was Bess Crawford. I answered, "It's Elspeth. I've just brought a convoy of wounded to London. I think I'm dead on my feet."

Bess laughed. "So did I, and then I had to travel on to Gloucestershire. Go to bed, I'll see you in the morning."

I wished her a good night and walked quietly to my room. Sitting down on the bed, I took stock.

There was nothing more I could do. I'd said that outside the station, but it was brought home to me now, sitting in the flat with no hope of reaching Rochester.

I tried to sleep, but sleep wouldn't come. And then it did, and when I opened my eyes again, it was morning.

I went to Victoria Station and begged for a ticket to Rochester. But travel was limited to essential personnel. With a straight face, I said to the elderly ticket master, "Please, I'm assigned to a hospital there. If I don't arrive in time to take up my duties, I'll be in such *trouble*. You don't know Matron—"

It was not difficult to leave the impression I was close to tears. I was worried enough to cry from sheer frustration.

In the end, he gave me a third-class ticket, all that he had, and I found myself in a carriage filled with young recruits on their way to France and their first test of battle. They laughed, played cards, wrote letters, sang songs to the tunes played by a corporal with a mouth organ. He was no more than one and twenty, I thought, his face still young but his eyes already old. I'd seen that look before, in battle-weary troops trying to hold on against desperate odds. He was on his way back to the nightmare that was war, but he said nothing of that to the untested men around him.

They skipped several verses of one song they were singing—in respect to my presence—but I thought, *who can blame them for making up verses about finding love in France?* Most of them will die before their next birthday, and never find love at all. Or if they survive, mutilated, how many will wed their sweethearts or the girls they dream about? One man from Staffordshire carried a photograph of Gladys Cooper, the actress. No sweetheart for him, and probably just as well.

He said to the soldier who sat next to him, gesturing to

the photograph, "Reckon she'll come over there and sing for us?"

There was a roar of laughter, and the young soldier flushed. "Well, what do you think, Sister?" he appealed to me.

"I think there's a very good chance," I agreed. He nodded, pleased, and then they were singing again.

I got down from the train in Rochester, asked directions to the hospital, and rather than wait for a cab, I walked to it.

I wasn't sure what I was going to find. The exercise helped to steady me.

There were patients in the wards and in the passages as well, and the harassed staff paid little or no heed to me. I searched quietly, carefully. Peter was not there. Not in the wards. Not in the passages. I had the most dreadful feeling he was dead. I finally found my way to the surgical ward, and Matron, pausing as she prepared to attend the next surgery, asked if she could help me.

"You aren't one of our Sisters," she said with some certainty.

I told her, "I'm searching for a patient, Captain Gilchrist. He's a friend of the family," I added, for fear she would jump to the conclusion I had a romantic interest in finding him. "I was told he could be in hospital here. I promised his brother I'd look in on him."

"You're on leave, then?"

"From France. I must go back tomorrow."

Nodding, she said, "He's just come out of surgery. And he did very well, I must say. Five minutes, Sister. No more."

My relief was almost a physical blow, and I had to look away for fear Matron would see how much those five minutes mattered.

Fervently thanking her, I went to the recovery ward she indicated, and halfway down the double row of cots, I discovered him. He was still unconscious from the ether, his face pale, his dark hair brushing his forehead, his beard noticeable, a black shadow that emphasized his pallor.

I drew up a chair and sat by his bed for a moment, then reached out and took one of his hands, holding it in my own. The fingers were well shaped, strong, the nails short.

"Are you there, Peter?" I asked softly, so that my voice wouldn't carry to the cot next to him. I knew, from my training, that he couldn't possibly hear me so soon. "You must get well. Are you listening? I want you to live more than anything in this world. I haven't told you about Alain. I couldn't. And as long as he's a prisoner, I can't abandon him. You'd understand that, I know you would. But I can't put you out of my mind. And even though I know it's wrong, I also know that it won't do any good to try. It's a muddle, and I don't know how to find my way out of it. Live for me, Peter, and we'll work—"

I broke off, hearing the Ward Sister coming toward me. I put Peter's hand on the coverlet again, where I'd found it, and turned to face her.

"Are you a relative?" she asked, and I knew from experience what she was about to say.

"The Captain is an old family friend. Indeed, he's like one of my own cousins. I don't suppose that counts."

"I'm afraid not."

I rose. "Will you tell me what his prognosis is?"

"If he survives the next four and twenty hours, we expect him to live. We had no choice but to operate, even though he'd already lost a great deal of blood. The infection was spreading. His recovery will be very slow at best. We can't operate again. If this surgery didn't improve matters, then there's nothing more to be done."

It was a grim prognosis. I felt my heart sink like a stone. I said, "Thank you for being honest."

She smiled. "I expect you'd guessed as much, Sister."

I hadn't. I'd been too intent on telling Peter what troubled me. I felt ashamed that I'd put myself first. And yet—and yet—I knew I had had to say what I did, for my sake if not for his. Even if he wouldn't remember, even if he died without waking, I'd told him the truth.

"You must leave," the Sister added. With a last look at Peter, I walked away.

It was one of the hardest things I'd ever done in my life.

• *Chapter Eight* •

WHEN I ARRIVED IN FRANCE, I found I was well behind the lines in a hospital unit. Matron looked at my orders, then studied my face for a moment.

"Sister Douglas. Are you all right?"

I wasn't. I'd spent my leave searching for Peter, and I had got almost no sleep at all, snatching what rest I could when it was possible.

"Yes, Matron."

"Have you been ill?"

"No, Matron." I could see she was of two minds about believing me. And so I added, "I received unhappy news while on leave. A friend of the family has been severely wounded. My training makes it impossible for me to pretend that he'll recover. For all I know, he's already dead." My voice nearly broke on the last words.

"I understand, but I must remind you that you must put personal matters aside if you are to work with the wounded. If your mind is wandering, you will not be able to make decisions quickly and efficiently. You were told that in your training."

"Yes, Matron. Only, then, before someone close to my family was wounded, it was easier to believe it was possible to put personal feelings aside."

She sighed. "My own brother has gone missing. He's in the Buffs. They've taken heavy casualties. But I mustn't put that above my duty."

I knew she was right. And if she could manage to carry on, then I would have to find a way.

"I'm sorry, Matron. It was wrong of me to bring my feelings back to France with me. You can count on me to do my duty."

Smiling, she said, "You're very young, Sister Douglas. But an excellent nurse from all reports. I'm sure I can depend on you."

And indeed, I found that throwing myself into my work helped. I also made certain I was too tired to dream or lie awake worrying. That helped too. But that night I kept my promise to the Gilchrist piper.

I tried to couch my news in the best terms possible, telling the truth but at the same time leaving the door open to hope. There would be no way of knowing if my letter would even reach the piper, but it was important to try.

Not twenty-four hours later, another letter found me, this one from Madeleine. She wrote that young Henri was thriving, and that despite the shortage of food in Paris, she was managing to feed the household.

And I've heard from Henri again. He says he has seen you, and that you are in good health. I'm so glad to hear it, dear Elspeth. I've been very worried about you.

There's been no word from Alain, but we have learned that he was wounded in the shoulder and could lose his arm if the infection doesn't respond. Henri is trying to have him released in some sort of prisoner exchange, since he has been so ill. But so far this has not come to pass. He killed quite a few of the enemy before he was captured, and the Germans could well see this as a reason to keep him. I am so worried for Alain and for Henri. I wish this wretched war was over and we could all be happy again.

I could sympathize with her. All of us had hostages to Fortune in this war. I prayed that Alain would keep his arm. Amputations were not always successful, and I couldn't bear to lose him too. He enjoyed tennis, golf, driving. Losing these, losing his independence would be inconceivable to him. I wished there was a way I could reach him and tell him that I thought about him every day and wanted him to come home safely. To raise spirits that must already be low as he fought to save his arm.

I replied to Madeleine as soon as I could, reassuring her that all would be well with Alain and Henri. That she mustn't worry too much and make herself ill. Advice she wouldn't take, I was sure, but I had to give it for the baby's sake.

There were, sometimes, exchanges of prisoners. If anyone could arrange such a thing, it would be Henri. He had been liaison to the British forces when last I saw him, and I wondered just how much he could achieve from our lines.

Dr. Higgins was a good man, and he spent long, arduous hours trying to save men who should have been given up for dead. I watched him work miracles, and I thought each time that here was someone's loved one given a chance to live. I wished that Alain and Peter had the same care, and waited for word that never came. Not from England. And not from France.

I was in the middle of sorting the incoming wounded when the Gilchrist piper came limping out of the dawn brightness, his eyes scanning the lines of wounded, the stretcher cases, the Sisters busy with bandages, jugs of water, and containers of septic powder. He spied me just as I turned to the next man, and I straightened, feeling such a sinking feeling in my heart that I could hardly breathe.

I turned away, not wanting to know what he had come to tell me.

I finished assessing a shattered foot, and by that time the piper had made his way to me.

"Is there news?" he asked in Gaelic.

"Did you receive my letter? Good, I'm glad. I've heard nothing more," I responded in the same language, and I saw the expression in his eyes as he turned to look toward the first hint of a rising sun.

"I have a verra' heavy feeling here," he said, and touched his chest with his fist.

"You've left your lines," I said, concerned for him.

"I brought in three wounded men," he told me, then added, "I volunteer every time, in the hope of news."

"The Captain is in England," I told him. "I'm not likely to hear anything. But I'll send word if I do. In a letter and by the walking wounded." For they were treated and returned to the lines as quickly as possible.

"Aye, that 'ud be verra' fine." He touched his cap, turned and walked away, heading for the trenches.

I watched him go. It was a measure of his devotion to Peter that he wouldn't give up. I admired him for it and wished that I'd heard something that would give him hope.

It was not long after that when an officer walked into the surgical ward, asking for Matron. I was bending over a patient, changing a bandage, when I looked up in time to see him frown.

I recognized him at once. It was the irascible Major who had sent me away from Peter and put me into a lorry for Rouen.

"I know you," he said, stopping in front of me.

I wasn't going to help him remember. I didn't like him, and I saw no reason to refresh his memory.

"After I sent you to Rouen," he said, finally placing me, "I realized why your face was familiar. You're that man Douglas's daughter. Lady Elspeth Douglas. I've seen your photograph in one of the society gazettes."

I looked quickly around, but none of the other Sisters were within earshot.

"Did you know my father?" I asked, trying to direct the conversation away from my title.

"Not at all. But I know your cousin. Kenneth Douglas. I was at Sandhurst when his eldest son was there."

Rory. "Have you had news of him?" I asked quickly.

"I have not. Does your cousin know about this?" He gestured to my uniform and the bloody bandage lying beside the fresh one.

I didn't know what to say. But he was waiting for an answer. I couldn't put him off. "I believe he does," I replied. For all I knew, that might be the truth.

"We'll see about that. I am not persuaded that your cousin would allow you to do this sort of work. I should have realized when I encountered you before that you were as headstrong as gossip says you are."

I said, trying to deflect what was coming, "My cousin is my guardian. I have done nothing to make him ashamed of me."

"So you say. Now where is Matron?"

"Major—"

But he turned away, and I knew I would only make matters worse by pleading with him.

"Matron has gone to the officers' ward," I said briskly. "You'll find her there."

Without a nod or word of thanks, he stalked out of the tent and disappeared.

I watched him go with a sinking heart.

What would Cousin Kenneth have to say? Not only about my training as a nurse but also about my failure to ask his permission? He took his role as my guardian quite seriously, and he was far more conservative than my father. He could very well see this as willfulness and insolence on my part, a lack of respect for his authority. It had been meant as nothing of the kind, but would he even listen to me?

I could only hope that Rory and Bruce would take my part and help me convince their father that this was the right thing to do. I was serving my country, just as his sons were, and I had not compromised my good name or my standards.

The Major must have left right after speaking to Matron, because I didn't see him when I went to the small canteen for my tea. And when I asked one of the other Sisters if she had seen him, describing him to her, she shook her head.

Matron didn't summon me later in the day, as I'd feared she would.

I sighed with relief and went about my duties with a lighter step. The Major had not said anything to her. I was sure of it.

And when I gave her my report on the condition of Sergeant Freeman, she made no mention of the Major.

I put him out of my mind and gave what comfort I could to the men in my care.

It was a week later when the letter arrived from London.

I was given leave to report to my superiors in the Queen Alexandra Imperial Military Nursing Service.

My heart sank. There could be only one reason for this summons.

When I arrived in London, I went to Mrs. Hennessey's house, freshened up after my journey, dressed in a carefully pressed uniform, and kept my appointment with my superiors. There the Matron in charge informed me that I had joined the Service without the consent of my guardian and that she had no choice but to ask for my resignation.

"I've been a very good nurse," I began, hoping to convince her that my skills were too valuable to lose, given the pressing need for trained nurses in France.

She cut me short. "You have been an exemplary nursing Sister," she told me. "But that isn't the issue here, is it? You did not give your title when you applied for admission for training, and you did not inform us that your cousin was your guardian. You told us only that your parents were dead and that you were your own mistress."

It was true. If I'd been a young orphaned woman of good family, I could have served my country. But for me it was not that simple.

Why had my father insisted in his will that my cousin Kenneth serve as my guardian until I was thirty? Had he been so unsure of my good sense? Had he been afraid that I would marry unwisely, or throw away on mad extravagances the fortune my mother had left me?

Or had he written his will when I was very young, and his protectiveness was a measure of his love for his motherless daughter?

"I can't believe that my guardian would insist on such a step. Perhaps if I speak to him—"

"If you wish, of course. But I must insist on your resignation before you leave here today."

I stared at her, wishing I could find the right words to

change her mind. It didn't matter to her that I was Lady Elspeth Douglas, accustomed to having her own way. I was the young woman who had broken the rules.

And rules were important to the dignity and the authority of the Service.

I handed in my resignation, feeling close to tears, but too proud to let them fall. I was asked to return my uniforms and identification and insignia by messenger. And then I was escorted by a young Sister out of the Service's headquarters and the door closed with finality behind me.

This had been my achievement, something that I had earned not by hereditary right but through my own efforts. It was something that I had been very proud of. Something more important than what to wear to the next party or dinner or ball.

It wasn't as if I'd chosen the theater or run away with an unscrupulous fortune hunter. I hadn't sullied my family name.

My hurt feelings turned to anger. It seemed so terribly unfair. Cousin Kenneth had inherited my father's title, my home, everything that had been mine when I was a child, even into young womanhood. And now he had taken this as well.

I wanted to hate him. And I found that I couldn't, which seemed much, much worse.

I went back to Mrs. Hennessey's flat, boxed up my uniforms, and carried them back to the Service, handing them over personally. They had been too much a part of my life to send them by post or by messenger.

And then I packed a small valise with just the things I needed, and went to find myself a seat on the next train to Scotland.

The house where I'd grown up was not far from the glen where the clans had mustered to fight for Bonnie Prince Charlie.

My father had taken me there as a child and shown me the wildly beautiful stretch of water and the long empty valley.

"Imagine," he'd said, standing on a knoll and pointing down to the valley, "hundreds of clansmen, led by their chiefs, marching in to camp alongside the loch, the smoke from their cook fires hanging low over the water. And as they came, the Prince watched. He spoke no Gaelic, he'd been brought up in France, his mother was Polish, but he was brave enough to put his life at risk to claim his rightful place on the throne of England and Scotland. Tall, fair, blue-eyed, surrounded by chieftains who were willing to put themselves, their people, and their fortunes at his disposal. It must have been a glorious sight, Elspeth. And yet no one has painted the scene. Can you believe that? Because we lost the fight, we were defeated and chased and captured and killed for traitors, and no one wished to remember the nightmare that followed."

And I had imagined the chieftains in their kilts, the sweep of eagle feathers in their bonnets, their retinue around them, the pipers with their bagpipes, sunlight flashing on swords and silver buckles and great cairngorm pins at their shoulders that held their plaids in place in a graceful fall down their chests. Serious business, a revolt against a sitting king, rightful king or no, but the clansmen laughed and boasted and told tales around their campfires of daring deeds and black betrayals.

I'd never forgot that magical moment, and as the train pulled into Glasgow, and I went to find a carriage to take me on the rest of my long journey, I listened to the voices around me, in English and Gaelic, and saw how many of the men were in uniform and how many others were stepping off the train from London with heavily bandaged arms and heads and even legs, crutches tapping across the platform toward the gate. I could see the cost of war here as well as in London and at all the stops we'd made between there and Glasgow. I wondered, not for the first time, if in Berlin or Wiesbaden or Munich there were walking wounded reminding the populace that war had come home to them, even if they had not been invaded.

I fell asleep in the carriage, the horses making good time in spite of a heavy rain. There was snow on the distant peaks, white caps that stood out against the gray skies, and I knew the way even in my sleep, the hollow sounds as we crossed bridges over rills and streams, the feel of the long pull up hills and the brisk trots down again. It wasn't long until I could see the castle in the distance.

It wasn't a castle in the ordinary sense, but a great house nearly overshadowed by the tower ruins that marked the earliest building here. I'd clambered and played over those ruins as a child, with a clansman and my nursemaid hovering to make certain that the laird's only daughter came to no harm. And my governess, trying to teach me decorum, had to struggle against the pull of the hills surrounding us or the stream that watered the valley, where I sometimes ran free of a summer, barefoot in spite of her best efforts to keep me shod, and ruining more than one dress playing with anyone who could be dragooned into joining me. It was a wonderful childhood. I was happy with the house in Cornwall—it was, after all, my very own—but it held few memories compared to the ones that overwhelmed me as I stepped down from the carriage and handed my valise to Geordie, who had hurried out to meet me.

The door stood wide, and I went into the Great Hall, with its enormous fireplace and the array of pistols and daggers, targes and spears, muskets and rifles that decorated the walls. This room had always been the first sight anyone had of Douglas Castle, the proud Scottish heritage on display. Beyond were the formal rooms and family quarters with their fine furnishings and collections of paintings and china and silver pieces. There was another house in Ayrshire and a town house in Edinburgh, but this was where I had lived most of my life.

I walked through the Hall, climbed the stairs to the passage where my father's study had always been, and took a deep breath before tapping lightly on the door, then opening it.

My cousin Kenneth was sitting at the ornate desk that had once been my father's and he rose in surprise as I came into the room.

"Elspeth!" he exclaimed, and came forward to take my hands in his and kiss me on the cheek. "Welcome home." He was a tall man, that flame red hair seeming to light the room, and his eyes were as blue as the sea. "Catriona will be sorry to have missed you. She's in Edinburgh at present with her sister, whose son John has just been reported killed in action."

"I'm so sorry to hear that. How sad."

He held me at arm's length. "You look tired. Was it an arduous journey? I'd have sent the railway car for you, if I'd known."

I shook my head. "Nothing is quite the same, these days."

"You're right on that account. Come in. I was just finishing a letter to Rory."

"What's the news of him?"

"He's well—or was, at the last writing. And Bruce is in York, where the doctors are still finding fault with his recovery. He will go mad before they've finished."

"But he's all right—he's taking the end of his war well?"

"As well as we can expect. It hasn't been easy for him, but I thank God on my knees every night that he's safe."

"I understand."

"What's the news from London? I closed the house, as you know—there wasn't enough staff to keep it open. All the men off to fight, and the younger women taking on war work."

"As I had done," I said. "Until you intervened."

He smiled. "Elspeth. It was best. Truly. Before word

got out. You aren't a housemaid who decides to nurse the wounded and dying."

"Nor are most of the young women who were Sisters working beside me. They came from good families. Bess Crawford's father held the rank of Colonel in one of the best regiments. Diana's parents are gentleman farmers, and Mary's parents are gentry as well. We could invite any of them to dine, and they wouldn't embarrass us by using the wrong fork or introducing unsuitable topics at the dinner table."

"That may well be, but you could look to marry the highest in the realm. And it wouldn't be suitable for you to have served in the Nursing Service."

"I'm not interested in marrying a prince of royal blood. And the man I would consider taking for my husband would be proud that I'd served in the war. Ask Bruce or Rory, if you don't believe me. They have both been treated by Sisters at the Front. They can tell you what it means to have trained hands assisting the doctors and saving lives."

"I'm sure they could. But it's not the place for Lady Elspeth Douglas. There are others who can do that service and do it well."

"Indeed? What *is* the worth of Lady Elspeth Douglas? What can she do save marry well, conduct herself properly as her husband's wife, entertain his guests, see to the care of his children, and make a good impression on everyone, indicating that she's well bred and above reproach?" I hadn't meant to lose my temper, but his words had stung. Was he hoping I might marry the Prince of Wales? Ridiculous.

"And what, pray, is so wrong with that? Catriona has been all those things, and I think she would say, if she were here, that she's been perfectly happy."

"Has she? Have you ever wondered? Or asked her? When this war is over, I shall bring someone here to ask you for my hand in marriage. And he will not care if I have been a nurse. On the contrary, he will be quite proud of what I have done for my King and my country."

But would Alain be proud? a little voice in my conscience asked. Henri had been surprised, and Madeleine had been shocked. To tell truth, I couldn't be sure how Alain would feel.

Still. Peter had understood. He had wanted to see me back in England, out of harm's way, but he hadn't been appalled to find me in uniform. Come to that, neither had Rory or Tommy Nesbitt.

"Who is coming to ask for your hand?" Kenneth asked abruptly.

"Alain Montigny."

"He shouldn't have spoken to you before he talked to me."

"He hasn't. He has only asked if I would permit him to call on you."

"And how do you feel about Montigny?"

"It's a proud name. The de Montigny family was one of the oldest in France, before the Revolution. Alain is a man I respect and care for deeply."

"You haven't mentioned love," he said. My cousin Kenneth was nothing if not sharp.

"I believe I love him," I said.

"It was you who told me that love mattered," he reminded me.

"And so it does. Just like nursing."

"Does it mean so much to you?" Cousin Kenneth asked, his expression quite serious. "I can't quite comprehend how you could feel so strongly about it."

"More than I can say. More than you can imagine. You sent your sons off to war, knowing the risks. Why should you be so unwilling to allow your cousin the opportunity to do her part? I have not lessened my worth as a wife, just because I have bound up amputated limbs and held the dying in my arms and written letters for a man blinded by shrapnel." I kept my voice steady, without accusing inflections. He had asked—and I had tried to answer.

Watching his face, I could see that he was still mystified.

"If you were my own child, perhaps I would have given my consent. But I stand in place of your father, and I must look not to my wishes but to what's best for your future. I'm sorry, Elspeth. I can't let you return to nursing."

I wanted to argue, but I knew it was useless. Instead I got to my feet.

"And that's your final word?"

"I'm afraid it is."

I nodded. "I'll stay the night, if you will allow me to. Tomorrow I'd like to go on to York, to visit Bruce."

"Of course I'll allow you to stay. It's still your home, Elspeth. You must know that."

"And I *am* a little tired. I think I'll go up to my room now, if you don't mind."

"Shall I ring for Mrs. Cummings?"

"Thank you, I can manage."

And I left him then. I knew I had to put a little space between us before dinner. I couldn't go on and on arguing for my way. He had made his decision, and to quarrel with him would only prove that I didn't know my duty.

I had learned much about duty, in Queen Alexandra's Imperial Military Nursing Service.

But that didn't mean that I'd given up. Far from it.

• *Chapter Nine* •

THE NEXT MORNING I SAID good-bye to my cousin over breakfast and soon afterward left for Glasgow and the train south and across England to York, changing twice.

Mrs. Cummings said as I went out the door, "Do na' fash yeresel' o'er this business of the nursing, my lady. It's for the best, I'm sure."

I thanked her and promised to come again soon.

But as the carriage left the drive and turned toward Glasgow, I knew that until this disagreement with my cousin was settled, I wouldn't come back.

Of course, my cousin saw it as settled—his way. I was just as determined to have it settled in the end my way.

I wasn't my father's daughter for nothing.

York was crowded, busy. I was directed to Laurel Hill, a country house just south of the city. It had been turned into a convalescent hospital for leg wounds. I presented myself to the Matron in charge, and she smiled when I added that I was a cousin to one Lieutenant Bruce Douglas.

"I'm so glad you've come. He needs cheering up. His leg has not been healing as well as it should, and so he isn't able to use crutches as often as he would wish. He's quite a favorite with the staff, and we'd like to see him in better spirits. Sister Clayton will take you to him."

Bruce was in a part of the house that had once been the billiard room. It had been partitioned in half, and a young Sister was trying to help him through the difficulties of handling crutches. He couldn't get the hang of it, his balance out of kilter. As I stood in the doorway watching, he swore and flung the offending crutch across the room, nearly toppling himself to the floor in the process. It was the patient Sister who caught him, scolded him for his language, and guided him to a chair.

At that moment, he recognized me. His face flushed to the roots of his red hair. It was a darker shade than his father's or Rory's, more what was called auburn, and the flush stood out on his fair skin. His dark blue eyes were nearly black with anger. He hadn't cared to have a witness to his pain.

"Hello," he said gruffly, straightening up. "What brings you to York? Rory told me you were in France."

"I'm so happy to see you," I said lightly, "that I'll ignore your rudeness. You can't imagine how worried we were for you."

"Yes, well, there are times when I wish—" He broke off, but I knew what he was on the point of admitting, that he wished he'd died rather than survived.

I came in and took the chair next to his. The Sister had

picked up the offending crutch and set it by him, then with a nod to me, walked out of the room to give us a modicum of privacy.

"I *was* in France," I said, making an effort to ignore his comment because I wasn't sure how to respond to it. More than one soldier I'd tended had expressed such a death wish. Most of them were amputees, but not all. *Not coming back whole* was dreaded more than dying. I'd always found words of comfort, but this was my favorite cousin, and I felt my throat close over them.

"You're on leave? This is a dreary place to spend it."

I hadn't intended to burden him with my troubles, but his mood was black, and it would do him good, I thought, to see that he wasn't the only one feeling down.

"Your father decided that it was unsuitable for a Douglas to be a nursing Sister and he informed the Service that I had not had his permission to train. I hadn't used my title, you see, when I applied. I'm sure it appeared that I'd joined under false pretenses."

He stared at me. "Is that true? You hadn't asked his permission?"

"I had a feeling he wouldn't approve."

Bruce laughed then, the lines in his face easing. "Dear Elspeth! You are your father's daughter."

I was torn between pleasure at his laughter and irritation at his amusement at my expense.

"It isn't something I find entertaining," I said with mock severity.

"No, of course not," he replied, his blue eyes still merry.

"You *are* good company," he added. "I've missed you, truly I have." He put out his hand, and I took it. "It hasn't been easy being wounded," he went on. "I sit here and brood over what I can no longer do, and then I try these damn—these infuriating exercises, but there's no improvement. I'm still helpless."

"Impatient man! It takes time for muscle and bone and tissue to heal. You can't expect miracles overnight."

"I never found sitting and doing nothing very pleasant—unless I'm reading. I want to be out and about. Well, I can hardly go stag hunting on crutches, or even walk the bounds with the ghillies. Which reminds me, MacLachlan's son was killed at Mons. I was there. And I was glad that his father was already dead."

MacLachlan the piper.

His son had not inherited his father's genius with the pipes, but he was a respectable piper, and he'd joined the regiment to be with Bruce, my cousin told me. I was saddened by the news.

The Sister appeared in the doorway, ready to resume Bruce's exercises. I sat and watched as under my eye, trying to prove he could do them, my cousin gamely went through his paces. Stretching and tightening the muscles in his leg, moving the foot first this way and then that, and standing by a table trying to rise on his toes and then down again, he clenched his teeth against the discomfort and made no complaint.

When he had finished, the Sister took him off to put cold pads on his legs, and Matron, who must have come to the doorway at some point, said, "You're good for him, Lady Elspeth. I haven't seen him so cheerful—and cooperative— since he arrived. He was quite down, then, and in a great deal of pain. Have you ever considered nursing? You have the knack for it, you know. Encouraging, keeping his mind off his disappointment at his slow progress, applauding when he accomplished his tasks. It's a gift."

I was so pleased at her praise. "I *was* a nursing Sister," I told her. "But my guardian disapproved."

"A shame, if I may say so. But then some men are still of the opinion that skilled nursing is best left to the lower classes. Would you be free to come again and work with your cousin? It would make such a difference."

"I'd be happy to," I told her, for I had intended to leave tomorrow for Rochester. Here was an excuse to put it off for another day, perhaps two. If Peter had lived, then there was time. If he had not, then I was in no hurry to find out.

I took a room in the village, and on my first night wrote to Mrs. Hennessey, begging her to keep me on at the flat while I spent a little time with Bruce as he recovered.

I knew she wouldn't understand why I wasn't in France or at one of the new clinics that were opening up all over England. I couldn't bring myself to tell her the truth, that I'd been dismissed. After a bit, when I'd grown used to the news myself, I could go to London and explain in person.

And so it was that I spent the next few days working with Bruce, cajoling, ordering, daring, promising, and even joining him in his exercises. He was on the point of managing his crutches when the letter came from Mrs. Hennessey in response to my own.

I'm so happy to hear from you, my dear, she began, then gave me news of Bess and Diana and Mary. She added, *There has been a letter for you. Shall I send it on to Yorkshire or will you be coming back to London when your leave is up? It's fortunate that you were able to spend it with your dear cousin.*

Maddeningly, she hadn't told me who had written to me. Mrs. Hennessey was convinced that to read letters addressed to someone else was the height of rudeness, and she included in that interdiction even looking at the name of the sender.

I hurried back to my room that night and wrote again to her, asking her to send the letter on to me in care of the inn in the village. I could have gone directly to London, but I'd finally worked up my courage to travel to Rochester.

Was it from Alain? Or from Madeleine with news of her brother and Henri?

Bruce was making good progress, and I was beginning to take note of a budding friendship with the Sister in charge of his therapy. Where they had been at odds over his behavior, now they were working in tandem, and his enthusiasm returned with each small conquest. He would never walk without a cane. I knew that now, the muscles and nerves having been terribly damaged and then neglected when he was taken prisoner. But I could see that it was only a matter of time before he could cast off his crutches.

Matron, inviting me to take tea with her in her small

office, said, "You must know how much your presence had brightened the lives not only of your cousin but of the other three officers who are working with Sister MacLeod. They are eager for your approval too. If you ever convince your guardian to let you return to the Service, I shall be happy to give you a good recommendation. It would please me no end."

I thanked her, but I was fairly certain that Cousin Kenneth was immovable on this subject.

On Friday evening I found a letter waiting for me when I returned to the inn for my dinner. The innkeeper's wife, delighted to have a titled lady in her humble inn, curtseyed to me as if I were the Queen herself, and said, "Your ladyship will be ready to dine in half an hour?"

"Yes, that would be lovely," I told her, as I had done every evening since I'd taken rooms here.

"And the post has brought another letter for you, which I have taken the liberty to leave on the little desk in your room."

"A letter?" I hurried up the stairs.

I could see before I had even reached the desk that my letter had not come from France. Disappointed, I picked it up and looked at the handwriting. No one I knew, I thought, for it was very round and feminine and unfamiliar.

I removed my hat and my coat, set them in the wardrobe, changed into a proper gown for my dinner, and then picked up the letter, opening it.

Dear Elspeth, it began, and I frowned. Had it come from one of the Sisters with whom I'd served? Apparently, I thought with a sigh, gossip had picked up the story of Sister Douglas and spread it to France.

> *I am not able to write to you, and so Sister Dennis has kindly suggested that she write for me. The muscles in my right arm are still quite stiff, and the chest wound has proved to be a nuisance, dragging on and on until I am sure to die of boredom long before it has finally healed. I am learning to write with my left hand, and to feed myself as well, but it is not a pretty sight. Sister Dennis has just told me that I have shown remarkable improvement, but I know she is being kind. I need to leave this place and learn to fend for myself. The doctors have forbidden me to travel to Scotland, but I think I could persuade them to allow me to go to Cornwall, if you are agreeable. I wouldn't be surprised to find that the house is closed for the duration, and if that is the case, I withdraw my request. As you have your lodgings in London, I won't be trespassing on your leaves, and I require little in the way of staff. A man to help me with my dressing and my exercises, and a cook-housekeeper. Do let me know if this is feasible.*

And it was signed, *Yours, always, Peter.*

I sat there, feeling as if a weight of stones had been lifted from my shoulders.

Peter. *He had lived.* I felt like dancing around the room, throwing caution to the winds. If life gave me no other gifts, this one would suffice until my last moments.

It was several minutes before I was calm enough to re-read the letter.

The house in Cornwall was indeed closed, only a skeleton staff to manage it. But Peter was welcome to go there, I would even take him there myself, if I could beg or borrow a motorcar. Anything to help him heal. For like Bruce, he was a proud man, and he would be anxious to get back into uniform as soon as possible, cursing every day of enforced idleness.

I was so relieved to know where he was, and that he was alive and well, that my hands were shaking as I fetched my letter box, intent on writing him at once and telling him that he was welcomed to the house in Cornwall, that I would see to it that his transfer there was by easy stages.

I dropped my pen in my haste, found it where it had rolled under the table, and then drew out a sheet of paper. As I did, something fluttered to the floor, and I nearly left it there in my hurry. But habit dies hard, and by habit I never left anything underfoot to trip a doctor or the stretcher bearers. I reached for it, was on the point of tossing it back into the letter box, and in the same instant recognized it.

It was the scrap of paper that Sister Blake had given me what seemed like ages ago, offering me her mother's house in Sussex as a refuge if I couldn't make it to London on a short leave. I'd never gone there—in fact, had foreseen no need to do so.

I slowly unfolded the scrap of paper and stared at it.

If I took Peter to Cornwall, I could find myself in the same predicament that had already cost me my place in the

Service. Someone would talk. A self-righteous servant, a villager, a visitor. The local doctor who would have the care of him, or his wife or nurse. I'd been burned once by self-righteous tattletales. How long would it take gossip from Cornwall to reach Cousin Kenneth's ears?

It was one thing to offer Peter the use of the house, for I was not living there. I had my lodgings in London. But if I visited Peter without what could be considered a proper chaperone, Cousin Kenneth would be shocked and angry. And rightfully so, even if we were innocent of any wrong-doing. Whispers about my conduct would be enough to cause irreparable damage to my reputation.

What's more I couldn't imagine how Alain would feel about that.

But in Sussex, who was there to gossip about the Scots officer and the Scotswoman who came to see how he fared? It would be so much simpler where no one knew us. I could always ask Mrs. Hennessey to accompany me on visits, and I would never stay overnight, even given her presence.

It seemed to offer the only way out of my dilemma.

I sat down, spoiled the first sheet with an enormous ink blot as my fountain pen leaked and I inadvertently smudged it.

Drawing out a second sheet, I collected my thoughts.

Dear Peter,

Alas, the house in Cornwall is indeed closed, with minimum staff. But there is a cottage in Sussex, and I'm sure that it could be staffed on short notice. Would that do? I am presently in York, where Cousin Bruce is recovering from wounds, but on my way south

It hadn't occurred to me to wonder which clinic Peter had been sent to. I recovered the envelope and looked. To my delight, it was just outside St. Albans.

I could come to you and make the necessary arrangements for a transfer there.

Would that be suitable? I have some leave coming to me, it won't be difficult.

But then how to sign it?

I could feel Alain's ring against my heart, and I felt a flush of guilt.

And so I signed it simply *Elspeth*. And when that was done, I wrote to the piper. I was sure Peter had done so already. But a promise was a promise.

I took both envelopes down with me to my dinner in the small private dining room the innkeeper's wife had set aside for me, and I asked if she would see that they were posted in the morning.

And what was I to tell Bruce, if I left so suddenly? He'd counted on me to be here for the weekend. I couldn't mention Peter.

I tossed and turned all night, my conscience troubling me and yet feeling the frustration of my situation every time I awoke and lay there, staring at the moon rising through the park of the great house where Bruce was convalescing. I wished I could speak to him, ask his advice before that letter went into the post in the morning and I couldn't retract what I had written.

Twice I rose and put on my robe, intending to go down and take it back.

But I couldn't talk to Bruce. Or anyone else. I had only myself to govern my actions. My own sense of self-worth, my honor, my father's memory to guide me.

As dawn broke, it occurred to me that Peter himself might not wish to come to Sussex. He could still choose to go to his brother in the glen where the ancestral house had stood for generations. His brother still lived there with his family, acting on Peter's behalf as laird until he came home again. Whatever the reason the doctors offered for not letting him take on such an arduous journey, I'd go with him and make certain he was all right.

As I fell asleep again, that thought followed me into my dreams.

• *Chapter Ten* •

WHEN I WALKED INTO THE clinic that morning, Matron was coming through Reception with an armful of patient records. She glanced up, greeted me, and then looked more closely.

"My dear, are you ill?"

I smiled and admitted that I'd slept poorly.

"Not worrying still about your cousin, are you? He's coming along famously."

"Yes, I'm so very pleased."

She said nothing more, but I knew she must think I was still grieving over the loss of my position with the Service. It was true, but it was not what had kept me awake all night.

And this morning, my letters had already gone by the time I came down for breakfast, the innkeeper's wife telling me quite proudly that she had taken them when she went to market.

As Caesar had said, the die was cast.

Bruce was waiting impatiently to show me what he had accomplished.

"Where have you been? Look—"

And he stood from his chair, held his cane at the ready, and took three steps toward me before I had to rush forward and catch him as he swayed.

"Damn," he said, more in frustration than anger. "I'd managed four just after breakfast."

I laughed and hugged him close. "My darling Bruce. I don't think I've ever seen anything quite so beautiful as those three steps."

"Sister MacLeod and I have been practicing in secret." He held me at arm's length and then frowned. "You look as if you've been crying."

"Just a sleepless night. I have those sometimes." I led him to the nearest chair and added, "I suppose you and I have one thing in common. We're both wishing we could turn back the clock."

"Matron has told me that she was impressed with your steadiness and devotion to patients. Would it mean so very much to you to return to France?"

"I made a difference. We all did, the doctors, the Sisters, the orderlies. I can't claim that I'm more skilled than the others, but I did what I could, to the best of my ability. Just as you did. And your father notwithstanding, I am proud of what I accomplished in such a short time."

One of the other convalescents came in just then, and Bruce greeted him with a remark about his crutches. Sister MacLeod joined us, and the exercises began. I watched and coached and laughed when I felt like crying at the bravery of Major Findley, who took his fall with his crutches in stride and got up to try again, in spite of his damaged arm.

The letter from Peter was quick in coming. I'd hardly expected my note to reach St. Albans, but by Monday the answer was waiting for me in my room.

The handwriting was the same as before, but the words were Peter's, and circumspect.

> *Give my best to Bruce, will you? I am grateful for your offer of the cottage and I hope it will be no trouble for you to take me as far as London. My motorcar is there, in the mews behind my flat. I'd stay there, but the flat is let to an officer seconded to the War Office for the next five weeks. A friend asked if I'd mind his using the flat, and at that time I wasn't sure I'd live, much less would have need of it myself. I look forward to seeing you very soon. You can't imagine how that will speed my recovery.*

It was signed with a roughly drawn *P* which I was certain Peter had done himself, to show that he was not quite the invalid I might have imagined. I smiled at the thought.

When I told Bruce that I must go to London, he took it with good grace.

"You've given me more time than I deserved," he said with an affectionate grin. "And you lifted my spirits no end, when I needed it most. Will you come back, when you can? I might well be able to walk to meet you."

"I shall, if I possibly can. At the moment, I'm not really sure what I will do with myself, but I'll think of something."

"You could go on the stage," Bruce said with a grin. "It couldn't be any worse than nursing."

An echo of my own thoughts earlier, just after I'd been asked for my resignation from the Service.

"It would serve your father right," I said tartly, and then apologized.

Bruce shook his head. "You've been hurt by his intractability. But then stubbornness is one of the family's most notorious traits. As you yourself know, to your cost."

"As if you were spared it," I said. "Remember my first day, when you threw your crutch across the room? It's a wonder you didn't break it."

He put his arm around my shoulders in a comradely gesture. "I wonder why you are my favorite female cousin?"

"That's easily answered. I'm your only female cousin."

Parting from Bruce was not easy the next morning. I was so grateful he was alive, although I couldn't say so. He wasn't ready to admit that he was glad he had survived. But I thought Sister MacLeod would soon make him realize that a lame leg was not quite the horror he had expected it to be.

In York I purchased a ticket for London, and when I arrived I went directly to Peter's flat. No one answered my knock at his door, and so I left a note saying that I'd taken the motorcar to St. Albans, where Peter required it.

I hadn't driven in months. Bruce had taught me to drive

Cousin Kenneth's motorcar, but he'd always been there beside me when I took it out for a spin. I was alone, now, and London traffic had increased tenfold, it seemed, since the war began in August. But I soon discovered that working the brake and the clutch came back readily as I set out for Mrs. Hennessey's house.

She was alone—none of my flatmates were in London at present—and so I could speak to her without giving away my plans.

I told her honestly what had happened about being forced to resign from the Service, saying only that my uncle had not seen fit to allow it, and that I was not of age yet, thanks to my father's will. I didn't mention the title.

She was astonished, putting her hand on my arm and saying with tears in her eyes, "How horrid for you, Elspeth, dear. What will you do now?"

"I should like to keep the flat until I decide," I replied. "Would you mind? I know there must be dozens of young women who would be grateful for it, but I don't think I'm quite ready to give it up."

"And why should you? There are other ways to serve, and you'll find something to your liking, I'm sure of it. Don't worry your head about that. And I won't say a word to my other lodgers. Not until you know your own mind."

It was so kind of her. I'd known a lot of kindness since I'd become "Elspeth."

She insisted on giving me tea, and we gossiped over it just the way we used to. I'd learned so much, living here. I truly considered it my home, despite the vast difference between my room upstairs and the large bedroom kept for me in Scotland. After my father's death, I had felt for the longest time that I had no home. Even Cornwall, where I'd stayed from time to time when I was a girl, had never seemed to be my home in the truest sense, because I was there so seldom. I'd found contentment and even happiness here in this simple house in Kensington, living in cramped quarters with three other women. Odd how such things can happen.

Before I left I gave her the direction for the house in Sussex. "I shan't be there long, only I must make certain that all is well before I leave. I'll stay in the village. Surely there's an inn or some such close by. But if a letter comes from France, will you please forward it at once? I'm so anxious for news. But don't tell anyone else where I am. I need a little time to think. Later, I could well ask you to come down with me, as my chaperone. Would you mind?"

She agreed, and I went out to Peter's motorcar with a feeling that all was well. I had written a letter to Cousin Kenneth, letting him know how Bruce was faring, and now I stopped to post it.

The man crossing the street in front of me was the same one I'd seen so many times before. And this time the package he was carrying away from the post office was a little larger than the one I'd found in my valise.

The looters were getting bolder. And coming as these did through this post office, where so many pieces of mail arrived and went out every day, it was less likely to be noticed. A village postmistress would become suspicious.

I was suddenly very angry. I could do nothing about what I suspected, but there was someone who could.

I drove not to St. Albans but to Scotland Yard.

It was an hour before an inspector came down to greet me, giving his name as Morgan. As he led me upstairs to his office, he said, "What brings you to the Yard? You were reluctant to discuss it with Sergeant Gibson."

"Because it's all based on suspicion," I said, waiting until he'd shut the office door behind us. I proceeded to tell him the saga of the Highland painting and what I'd discovered since then.

Inspector Morgan listened intently, and then when I'd finished, he sat there for a moment, as if considering what I'd said. I had the sinking feeling he might thank me for my information and send me on my way. People were seeing spies around every corner. Why not looters as well?

To my surprise he opened his desk drawer and took out a folder. Inside was a photograph, and he turned it around so that I could see it.

I studied it, uncertain where I'd seen the man shown there.

And then I remembered. "He was on the train out of Paris. He was just behind me and helped me with my valise. Sadly, he died of his heart before he reached Calais. I saw them take his body away on a stretcher to a waiting ambulance. Is he involved with those smuggling paintings into England?"

"I'm afraid he was one of our men. We've been hunting a ring of thieves. Sadly, the war has meant greater opportunities than theft. There's been quite a bit of looting, often in that brief interlude between the time owners flee and the Germans arrive. Dangerous work, but lucrative. And Inspector Davis didn't die of his heart. He was murdered. We haven't had a lead on who might have killed him."

I was shocked. "Murdered? That very nice man? How awful."

"Indeed. Now, you've given me the name of the shop where these items are taken once they've been picked up. But we'd like you to act as a spotter for us and point out the man we've been looking for."

It would mean waiting one more day—perhaps even two—before I would see Peter.

I hesitated.

"You'll be protected every step of the way," Inspector Morgan told me. "We need your eyes."

I took a deep breath. "Yes, all right."

The next morning, waiting in a cold rain in a shop near the post office, waiting for the unknown man to appear, we drank pots of tea. The next day there was a cold wind. The sergeant assigned to stay with me wore a plain suit of clothes, ill fitting, as if he had forgotten how to wear anything but his uniform. Even in the warmer shop, after a while I felt like stamping my feet to keep the blood circulating.

On the third day, I saw him. He wasn't going into the post office, he was walking past it. I told the sergeant what I thought.

"He must live out in that direction," he agreed, pointing

with his chin. "All right, Miss, I'm setting out to follow him. Yon constable on the corner will come over and see you safely to Kensington as soon as I step out the door."

"Will you tell me what happens? Whether I was right about this or not?"

He grinned. "You'll see it in the newspapers, Miss. When he's taken into custody. But we'll let him run a bit first. Leading us down the rabbit hole, like."

And then he was gone, cautioning me to stay where I was until the constable had come for me.

An hour later, I was on the road to St. Albans, relieved to have no more to do with murderers.

I found the clinic outside the town in a house called The Gables. It was a lovely old Elizabethan manor that had been turned into a hospital for critical chest cases. I could see the moment I walked through the door that it was well staffed and efficiently run.

A Sister greeted me as I crossed the threshold, and I asked if I could be taken to see Captain Gilchrist.

Her face brightened. "The Captain? Yes, if you'll come this way?"

I wondered if she was the Sister who had written Peter's letters for him, but she said nothing to me that indicated she knew who I was or why I had come.

Peter was in a small room just off the library. It appeared to have been a sitting room or morning room, now turned over to convalescent patients for reading, writing letters, or listening to music from the new machine I saw in one corner.

As Peter looked up, I was shocked by how thin he was, and how his face was lined with pain. He hardly seemed to be the same man, and I felt a rush of sympathy for him.

And then he smiled, that lovely smile that touched his dark eyes with such warmth that I felt myself flush.

"I can't rise to greet you," he said, indicating his wheelchair. "Sorry. You'll have to come to me." He held out his hand.

I crossed the room, my heart pounding, and gave him mine. He took it in his left and held it tightly. I knew what he was telling me without words, that he would have liked to say more and couldn't in the circumstances. There were patients, nurses, and orderlies everywhere one looked. There was no such thing as privacy.

"I've brought your motorcar," I said, taking a step backward and releasing his hand. "It might be far more comfortable for traveling than the train."

"It's very like you to think of that," he responded and then went on lightly, "You're three days' late. I was beginning to worry that you'd disappeared again. I didn't know you had a house in Sussex."

"I don't. It belongs to a friend. She offered it to me once, some weeks ago, if ever my leave was too short to reach London or Cornwall. It's a cottage, I gather, her mother's home. The important thing is that it has to meet whatever requirements the staff here has set out for your care." I smiled. "They will know best."

From his expression I didn't think he cared what the doctors had to say, but disregarding instructions could be just as dangerous as a relapse. I remembered Bruce throwing his crutch across the room and wishing himself dead because he couldn't walk yet.

Changing the subject, Peter said, "It's arranged that you'll dine here tonight." He seemed to take note of my civilian clothes. "You aren't wearing your uniform."

"Long story. It will keep. I must go and speak to Matron."

"I'll be here," he said, his gaze following me as I walked through the door.

I found Matron, had a long conversation with her, and then was taken to speak to Dr. Fuller.

He gave me much the same instructions as Matron had. Captain Gilchrist was not completely out of the woods yet and he had to mind what he did.

"He could still lose his arm if there's any additional infection. Important to keep the wound clean, the bandages fresh. And he shouldn't try to walk far until he's stronger. Too soon will only increase the danger of a fall. That could have serious consequences. Reinjuring his wound, opening an incision, even broken ribs piercing a lung. He's lost enough blood already."

There were other sensible cautions as well. Peter must drink fluids and eat well to replace the blood he'd lost. He must be very careful neither to overtax his strength nor overtire himself, nor must he use the arm until the exercises he'd been given had been carried out to the letter for several weeks. And so on, instructions that I had already anticipated. Peter would need a valet to help him dress and undress and he must report to the specialist in London after two weeks' time to be sure all was well.

"We're not eager to release the Captain. He's been a favorite here," Dr. Fuller ended. "But the bed is needed desperately for new cases, and he tells me you've had training as a nurse."

But I couldn't stay with Peter and watch over him. I would have to find someone who could.

The next morning, settled in the motorcar, Peter bade farewell to the staff of the clinic and the friends he'd made there. As I drove sedately down the drive and turned toward London, he said, "My God. I don't think I've had a moment alone since I was shot. I can't tell you how much I've looked forward to your coming."

We had both felt the constraints of the crowded clinic. I said, "It's good to see you again, Peter. I was so worried. In Calais. Dover. Rochester."

"You were there?" he asked, surprised. "I thought I'd dreamed hearing your voice."

"I was there." Even now I couldn't tell him how worried I'd been. "You fought a long hard battle to survive."

"So they tell me. I don't remember very much about it." He took a deep breath. "It's behind now. Thank you, Elspeth, for making it possible for me to leave the clinic."

We had fallen into our old way of going on together. Two people who felt at ease with each other, like old friends. Like lovers. At once comfortable and dangerous.

From there we drove on to Sussex to the village of Aldshot. I passed the time telling him about my resignation from the Nursing Service, forced by my guardian, about Bruce, even about my brush with crime and Scotland Yard. But not about Alain.

In turn he told me about his foster brother, now on the mend, about his piper, and about others in his regiment. But nothing about his feelings for me.

It was late afternoon when we arrived, and I was aghast at what we saw.

Save for the church, which gave it the rank of village, Aldshot was no more than a hamlet. It consisted of a road that looped back on itself in a rough figure eight, and there must have been no more than twenty houses all told. No inn, no doctor, not even a shop or bakery or ironmonger. Just houses and the farm buildings behind most of them.

But Walnut Tree Cottage was a lovely bungalow set back from the road and ringed by a neatly trimmed hedge. The brick was a warm rose in the dying afternoon light, and a walnut tree held pride of place in the front garden.

I said, "Peter, this will never do. We must go back to Midhurst, or some other sizeable town, and tomorrow I'll find something more suitable."

He said, "I don't think I could face another mile. Not without a rest. Is there anyone inside? There are no lamps lit."

I left the motor running and got down, walking up to the door. Underfoot I saw several walnuts lying in the brown grass, and I remembered what Sister Blake had said: *Bring me a walnut . . .*

Knocking at the door, I waited for someone to come. Just then a woman called from across the street, throwing a shawl over her shoulders as she hurried toward me.

"Did Sister Blake send you? I'm that sorry, I didn't know. The letter must have got delayed. We don't have a regular post here, not since the war, you know." She reached me and held out a key. "I did for Sister Blake's mother, when she was alive, and I keep an eye on the cottage for her. Was you intending to stay long, my dear?"

"You're Mrs. Wright?" I took the key and unlocked the door. The house was chill inside, I could feel it as I stepped into the short hall, then walked into the front room.

"Yes, indeed," the woman was saying as she lit the lamps. "Now, that's better."

As the first wick caught, I could see the hearth, carefully laid for a fire, and when the second lamp bloomed into light, I noticed that the room was immaculate, polished furnishings, an old but beautiful carpet on the floor, and a bowl of lavender making the air sweet. It all looked as if the late Mrs. Blake had just stepped out for the afternoon, and the house was waiting for her return.

Mrs. Wright was already kneeling by the hearth, striking a match and holding it to the kindling until it caught properly. As it fed on itself and the flames licked at the wood in the grate, the effect was quite cheerful.

"I don't think we can stay after all," I said to Mrs. Wright. "The officer in the motorcar has just been released from hospital. He will need more care than we can find here in Aldshot. I shall have to drive back to Midhurst. But first I think a short rest might be best for him, and perhaps some tea."

She smiled. "It's all right, Sister. I can prepare your tea, and a light supper, after. The beds are made up, the sheets are clean. And my husband can do for him, if he needs help. You needn't drive all the way back to Midhurst to-night. Tomorrow will be soon enough."

"He will require a doctor's care—"

"There's a very fine doctor in Midhurst. Baker is his name, Dr. Baker. He's nearing sixty, but a better man you'll never find."

Peter was still sitting in the motorcar in the cold. I said, "I must bring Captain Gilchrist in. Could you make our tea, please? Or is it possible for me to find what I need here?"

"I'll just run across to my house for a jug of milk, and there's a bit of cake left from our own tea, if you don't mind that it's already been cut into. Joel, my husband, can help you get the Captain down from the motorcar and settled."

She seemed set on having us stay. But it was impossible. I couldn't spend the night in the same house with Peter, it would be wrong. I thanked her for her help, and we closed the door to the front room to keep in what warmth there was while I went back to the motorcar.

Peter said, "What's happening?"

"You're to come down and rest for a bit. Mrs. Wright is bringing us tea, and her husband can help you inside."

At that moment, a man who must be Mr. Wright came out of the house and walked briskly over to the motorcar.

"Now, then, sir, we'll just get you out of there. Lean on me, I'll give you support until you can stand."

"It's my chest, not my legs," Peter said irritably.

"That's right, sir, but the legs get cramped, like, sitting for a long spell. From London, are you?"

As he spoke, he helped Peter from the motorcar, and together they walked up the path to the cottage door. I followed, wishing I'd brought Mrs. Hennessey with us, for I was beginning to think we might indeed have to stay the night after all. Peter was walking stiffly, holding his arm and shoulder carefully so as not to jar them. I watched him inside, and then Mrs. Wright was there, a jug of milk in one hand and a covered plate in the other.

We followed Peter and her husband into the cottage and made Peter as comfortable as we could in the front room. Mrs. Wright ran up the stairs to the bedrooms above and brought more pillows for Peter, gently helping to settle him without fussing. Then she disappeared into the kitchen.

"Where was you wounded, sir?" Mr. Wright was asking Peter, and I left them to it, walking to the room across the passage and finding that it boasted a piano. I ran my fingers over the keys, surprised to discover that it was in tune.

From there I went to the kitchen, small and compact. Mrs. Wright looked up. "Mrs. Blake's father owned much of the land hereabouts," she said, busy with the tea tray. "And she spent her summers here. She loved the cottage, she did. You can feel it, can't you? That it was a happy house, and cared for. Her daughter loves it too."

And it was true. There was an air about the cottage that

seemed to enfold us, welcoming us in spite of the cold that had seeped into the floors and the walls as summer faded.

"I come over and light a fire in the rooms once a week, to air them and keep things fresh. It's something I enjoy."

"Does Sister Blake often send—er—visitors here?"

"Once in a while. She likes to know the house is lived in again. Not just standing empty."

"Who planted the walnut tree?"

"That? Mrs. Blake's father planted it the day she was born. Walnut cake, that's what Mrs. Blake loved best. I made her one before she died, when she was too ill to do for herself. She ate every bit of it, and it gladdened me to watch her."

"You've known the family a long time," I said.

"Yes, that we have. My father did for the Blakes, and my mother was the housekeeper. Most of the other people in Aldshot worked the land or kept the horses or looked after the gardens in back. The manor house burned down a long time ago. The family kept the cottage and built another house in Pulborough. Sister Blake's mother married for love, and she said to me that it was the only thing that could take her away from here. And so every summer she'd come back for a month, just herself, and then her daughter, until the day her husband died. When that happened, she came home to stay. She said she couldn't bear to rattle around in that big house in Pulborough all alone. When she first came, I thought she'd die of a broken heart, mourning him. But the cottage brought her back to herself. It was something to see, how she slowly healed here. Mind you, she still missed him, but she knew she had to live on for her daughter, and that she did."

Picking up the tea tray, she smiled. "The kitchen is warming up already with the fire in the stove. I'll see that it's banked properly tonight, ready for breakfast in the morning."

"We can't stay," I said. "It wouldn't be proper. I'm his nurse, yes, but we aren't—married."

"You can sleep in my extra bedroom, if you like, and Joel will stay with the Captain. I don't see anything wrong with that."

I followed her into the front room. Peter was looking less pale, and I could tell that Mr. Wright had been telling him the history of the house, for he was describing the planting of the walnut tree as we came in.

Mrs. Wright set the tea tray on a table her husband brought closer to the fire, and then he disappeared as she poured out two cups of tea.

"We're about out of sugar," she said, "but the hives have flourished this year, and there's plenty of honey. I'll bring you a pot tomorrow, and see that you have a good breakfast."

Just then I heard the outside door open, and the next thing I knew, footsteps sounded on the stairs. Mr. Wright was bringing in our luggage.

"We can't stay," I began.

Peter said, "It will be all right, Elspeth. Wright here says you can take their spare room for the night. I don't think I could face getting back in the motorcar just now."

I could see the circles of pain under his eyes and the tightness of his jaw. I felt angry with myself for not having the wit to look at Walnut Tree Cottage myself before bringing him this far.

The fault was mine. I'd assumed that the cottage would be in located in a sizeable village where Peter would have everything he needed to heal. I was used to a different world, and I had misjudged this one.

I wanted to argue, to set my mistake to rights, but it would cost Peter more than he could face just now. My pride could wait.

I helped him cut up his slice of cake, noting that he handled his teacup left-handed with reasonable skill.

"If you'd prefer to stay," I said lightly, "then stay we shall."

He gave me a grateful look, then managed a smile. "Pretend it's the Petit Trianon."

The small château on the grounds of the Palace of Versailles where Marie Antoinette could escape the formality of the French Court and play at being an ordinary person. Her version, of course, of ordinary.

I laughed, pleased to hear him make light of his situation.

He dozed in his chair until supper was brought, and afterward, Joel Wright helped him up the stairs. I'd already turned down the bed while Mrs. Wright made up the fire and then prepared blankets on the floor for her husband. "He'll be close by if the Captain needs anything," she said, standing back to admire her handiwork. "There's another blanket if he wants it. And I've set a covered glass of water by the bed, if the Captain is thirsty in the night."

Mrs. Wright led me across the road to her house, far simpler than Walnut Tree Cottage, and apologized for the small, plainly furnished little room down the passage from hers, where I was to sleep. She had at first insisted that I should have their room, but I refused to allow it, saying that I would be perfectly fine in the spare room.

To my surprise, I was, and I slept well enough there.

Peter, on the other hand, had slept better in Walnut Tree Cottage than he had for weeks in the clinic.

"Even at night it was never quiet. A veritable chorus of snores, the sounds of coughing, men moaning in their sleep, some even crying out. I expect I was also tired, but it was a very good night."

Breakfast was served on the tea table, where I suspected that Mrs. Blake had also taken her meals, and then the Wrights retired to their own home for their breakfast.

"Did you manage last night?" Peter asked. "I was rather selfish, abandoning you to God knows what arrangements. But I don't think I could have crossed the road if my life had depended upon it."

"The spare bedroom is small but comfortable," I assured him. "And Mrs. Wright saw to it that I had everything I needed."

"Must we go back to Midhurst today? This is heaven, after the jolting on the roads. A day—two at most—and I can face anything."

"I got you into this," I said ruefully. "If you'd prefer to rest a bit, I can only let you have your way."

"It's a lovely little cottage." He was gazing about the room, noticing more than he'd felt like taking in the night before.

"Petit Trianon indeed," I said.

He laughed. "Mrs. Wright would be astonished to learn that an Earl's daughter slept in her spare room."

"Hush! They might come in and hear you."

"Don't worry, from where I'm sitting, I can see them the instant they leave their own doorway. I will say that Mrs. Wright is an excellent cook." He had had a good appetite for breakfast, according to Mrs. Wright, although there were still signs of pain and fatigue marking his face.

He held out a book. It was a Dickens novel. "I found this in the bookshelf upstairs. Read to me?"

I put more wood on the fire and then sat down again. "Are you sure you are comfortable here? We can't be sure the doctor in Midhurst is as good as Mrs. Wright suggests."

"I've been poked and prodded by doctors since I was wounded. I've had two surgeries, a long recovery, and more prodding and poking. This is bliss, this cottage. Better even that rattling around in my flat or your Cornish house. If I need to see a doctor, we can always find one."

He seemed to take it for granted that I would stay as well. At least for a few days.

And as if he'd read my mind, he said, "My dear, don't fuss. I've got you to keep up my spirits, Mrs. Wright to feed me, a comfortable chair and a comfortable bed, with

Wright to help me dress and undress. I've been a soldier long enough that I don't require a large house and a full staff of servants to manage my life. Where will you go? What will you do, when you leave here? Go back to London and fret over your cousin's interference? There's nothing you can do to change his mind, and by the time you're of age to make your own choices, the war will be a distant memory, and it won't matter any longer."

He was right.

But there was the other side of that coin. If I stayed here too long, I would find it harder to convince myself that I didn't love Peter Gilchrist. And that could never be. Just sitting across from him, enveloped in the warmth of his caring, listening to his deep, quiet voice offering me comfort, I had to fight my own desire to throw caution to the winds and stay at Walnut Tree Cottage forever.

We talked for a time, and I read to him until he fell asleep. Mrs. Wright had come in again, had made the bed upstairs, cleared away the breakfast dishes, and brought in our tea by the time Peter woke up.

"Sorry," he said, flushing a little. "Your voice is soothing, and I couldn't help myself. Poor company for you, sitting across from a sleeping man most of the morning."

"You aren't here to provide amusement for me," I said, taking his cup of tea to him, then returning to pick up my own. "Rest is a great healer."

"After my tea, if Wright can help me manage the stairs again, I'll do my exercises. Then perhaps we could walk a little."

He couldn't go far, and it wasn't good for his lungs to breathe in the cold December air. But it was the best way to regain his strength and increase his appetite.

We tried to walk a little farther each day, and sometimes one or the other of our neighbors would stop to speak to us, accepting us, Mrs. Wright told me, because we were staying in the Blake house. That, it seemed, was entrée enough for the local people.

We had come to a comfortable arrangement with the Wrights. They did the marketing and the cooking, the cleaning, and so on, and we paid them at the end of each week for what they had spent, although they were always reluctant to take anything for themselves. I finally had to tell them that Sister Blake had insisted that we must pay for services as well, and finally, shyly, they agreed to let us carry out her wishes.

It was difficult to spend my days so close to Peter. He said nothing more about his love for me. Before we'd come to Walnut Tree Cottage, it had been different, snatched moments in the midst of a war, Peter wanting me to know how he felt, what his intentions were. Here, where I was in his company hour after hour, he was careful never to make me uncomfortable, careful never to press his suit or in any way take advantage of our present circumstances. Even my guardian couldn't have expected more consideration from a suitor.

The problem was on my side. Peter's laugh, the way his eyes reflected his smile, his small kindnesses, his very presence, protective in every way, the sound of his voice from another room, quickening my pulse, knowing he was near, within call—these things and so many others wrapped me in happiness. I *felt* loved, and in the afternoons or after dinner, we would talk in that companionable way people do when they're content in one another's company.

I thought one evening as Peter and I sat by the fire, watching the flames leap into the chimney, red and gold at the heart, that Alain and I had never reached this stage in our relationship. We'd always been chaperoned, and so it had never been possible. Only on that last evening before he'd joined his regiment had we approached it, and it was all too quickly gone.

I knew I should leave. I knew it was unwise staying here, giving my heart away bit by bit. But the thought of going was insupportable.

One afternoon Peter came down the stairs wearing his officer's greatcoat and using the cane that Joel Wright had found for him in the village. It was old, the handle well rubbed by the hands of many people, and sturdy enough to support him properly.

We set out down the path. Looking up at the walnut tree, he said, "It's a pleasure to see a tree like that, after the blasted and blackened stubs of trunks I'd grown accustomed to in France."

"Yes, it must be beautiful in the spring, as the leaves come out." We wouldn't be here to see that, I thought.

He took my arm to counterbalance the cane, and I could feel the warmth of his body so close to mine. I wanted to move closer, cling to his arm, our heads almost touching as we talked. But I kept the proper distance, as I'd been trained to do as a Sister, assisting but in no way encouraging contact.

We walked as far as the church. Mrs. Wright had told us that the Rector was serving in France as a chaplain. He had left in November, and now the village was served for the duration by the priest in the next village over.

There was an interesting story to the construction of the church. According to Mrs. Wright, it had been built by a former resident of Aldshot who had feared for his immortal soul. One of Mrs. Blake's ancestors, he had left the village to seek his fortune, and gone out to India with Robert Clive. He had come home a nabob, but apparently his conscience bothered him—no one seemed to know quite why—and so he donated land as well as the money to build "a fitting church" in his birthplace. And in his will he had asked to be interred in "the foremost place before the altar." His wish was granted, but the general opinion of Aldshot was that whatever he'd done in India, it had taken more than the gift of a church to cleanse his soul.

Pausing, leaning heavily on his stick, Peter said, "I never thought to ask the Wrights. Where is the rectory?"

"Over there, I think," I said, pointing to a house across the road. "It has a lovely orchard. Do you see? Well pruned, healthy."

"The ancestral Blake's largesse didn't extend to the rectory," he commented. For it was no bigger than any other cottage in the village. "Either that, or the church had proved more costly than he'd imagined."

I smiled. "I'll ask Sister Blake, if I ever see her again."

Turning by common consent, we walked back the way we'd come, toward the cottage. Peter was unusually quiet, and I thought perhaps his ribs were hurting in the cold December wind.

Almost to the hedge that surrounded the front garden, he stopped, his gaze on the walnut tree.

I stopped as well, hoping the outing hadn't been too much for his strength. He still had good days and bad.

But I was wrong.

Without looking at me, he said, "We can't do this, Elspeth. I thought we could manage, but it won't work. I love you too much. And at present I can't speak to Kenneth. You must go back to London. But not today. Tomorrow . . ."

"Not today," I agreed, keeping my voice steady by an effort of will. "We'll leave tomorrow to itself."

He chuckled, deep in his chest, and I felt myself go weak in the knees. "Peter."

I wanted to tell him about Alain. Now. While I could.

"Don't," he said. "Don't say anything. Just give me your company. I won't ask for more, I won't tell you again that I love you. Friends?"

But I knew even as I repeated "Friends" that it would be impossible. For both of us.

We walked the rest of the way without speaking, and by the time we had come in and warmed ourselves by the fire in the hearth, Mrs. Wright was bringing in our luncheon.

• • •

We sat talking until quite late that night, keeping to topics that led us safely through the quagmire of emotion, and then I went across the street to rouse a sleepy Joel Wright to put Peter to bed.

As I went up the stairs to my own room, Mrs. Wright, standing in her doorway in her dressing gown, said, "He's such a lovely man, isn't he? The Captain? It's a pleasure to see to him. I hope he'll be staying on."

"I believe he will," I said, and wished her a good night.

The next day crept into another and then another. I knew it was best to return to London as soon as may be, but I put it off, night after night. And then one evening as I was preparing to go in search of Wright to help him upstairs, Peter called to me from the front room.

"Come and see, Elspeth. You won't believe what they've done!"

It was a bright, starlit night, clear and cold. As I went to the window to see what Peter was talking about, I drew in a breath in disbelief.

The walnut tree in the front garden was alight with candles at the end of its branches, each in a small saucer of paper, and the flames danced in the night air like something alive, blue and gold and white hot, a halo that set the tip of each branch aglow with warm light.

It was the most beautiful thing I'd ever seen. I stood

there, staring out at the spectacle, and suddenly I realized the purpose of the tree alight with the brightness of joy. It was Christmas Eve! I had lost track of time, and so had Peter.

He put his good arm around my shoulders, pulling me close, and we stood there together as the candles burned down.

And then he bent to kiss the top of my head.

"A happy Christmas, my love. May there be many, many more for us."

A tap at the door broke the spell, Wright come to see Peter to bed. We stepped apart, not looking at each other, and I said, "How late it is, I must go!"

I hurried out of the room as Wright came in, and walked through the light cast by the walnut tree, seeing it glimmer and glisten into bright rainbows through my tears.

•   *Chapter Eleven*   •

I HAD NO GIFT FOR Peter the next day. I hadn't expected to stay as long as this. But I'd already driven into the nearest village for gifts for the Wrights. These were intended to thank them for all their kindnesses, but they would do for Boxing Day just as well.

Mrs. Wright was at the foot of the stairs as I came down to my breakfast. In her hands was a small blue glass jar with a festive arrangement of ribbons around the top.

"A little something for you," she said, handing it to me.

"And this is for you," I said, holding out a silk scarf that matched the blue of her eyes. "I'm so sorry I had no paper to wrap it for you. And with it comes my gratitude for your many kindnesses to me."

"Never you mind about the paper," she said stoutly. "You've given Joel and me such happiness just watching the two of you together." And before I could answer, she led the way to the front room where my breakfast was always set out.

I opened the jar, expecting to find potpourri or a lotion made of herbs and rose hips, that sort of thing, and instead found it contained shelled walnuts from the cottage tree.

I was close to tears, staring down into it. She couldn't have known, could she, how much that tree had come to mean to me. And, I thought, to Peter as well. I'd already thanked her for the candles last night, as I came in to go to bed, and she had flushed with pleasure.

"It took half the village to get it done quickly and quietly," she told me. "We're so glad you liked it. Mrs. Blake had always put candles on the walnut tree for her birthday, from the time when it was hardly more than a stalk and a few limbs. Her father wouldn't allow her to light them, he did that himself. And Joel and I thought, Wouldn't it be fine to do it for a Christmas surprise?"

I put the lid back on the jar and set it beside my plate.

"Thank you, Mrs. Wright. That's the most thoughtful gift you could have given me. I'll always remember it."

"I'd send a jar to Sister Blake too, if I could, but she's always moving about and packets go astray, often as not."

I recalled my promise to Sister Blake—I owed her a walnut from that tree, as "rent." I would make a point to collect one that very morning, on my way across to the cottage.

When I got there, I found Peter in a very odd mood.

He reached into his pocket and took out a carefully folded handkerchief, handing it to me.

I opened it, and inside was a circlet of bone. It had been cleaned and polished and then engraved with what I quickly identified as tiny walnut shells. It must have taken hours and hours of work, and it was quite beautiful.

"I can't offer you a ring," he said. "Not until I speak to Kenneth. This is simply a gift between friends. I hope you will accept it as such." He grinned. "I wanted to give you something, and this was the only thing that came to hand. I don't expect you to wear it. Lady Elspeth Douglas would hardly go to a ball sporting a pig's bone."

Such a contrast to the ruby ring that Alain had given me. I could feel it on its chain around my neck, holding me to my promise.

After a moment, I said lightly as my fingers closed over the ring, "Peter, you shouldn't have. I'm overwhelmed by your extravagance." It took every ounce of my will to say that, but I managed it without tears.

"And so you should be. It was the devil to carve."

We laughed, and I put the circlet on my finger. To my surprise it fit.

I took it off again and set it carefully on the mantel shelf.

"Now I must have a look at your bandages."

Wright always replaced them perfectly, copying the way the doctors in St. Albans had put them on before Peter left their care.

The wound was healing well. I sprinkled it with septic powder, then rebandaged it. But when I asked him to lift his arm, he was unable to raise it beyond the level of his shoulder.

"The damn—the exercises seemed to have stopped working."

"Then it's time to take you to a doctor in Midhurst or Pulborough—even to London, if need be. He can order new exercises. Tomorrow is Boxing Day. The next day, then."

We agreed. And then I put it all out of my mind, trying to make the day merry. I saw the bone ring on the mantel shelf every time I passed. And yet I couldn't bring myself to put it on again. I knew Peter would have liked to see me wear it, if only for the day, but there was Alain. And I couldn't. Even for Peter.

On the day after Boxing Day I drove Peter to Midhurst. The doctor there, recommended by Mrs. Wright, examined him and afterward told me, "I'd be happier if he went back to his doctor in St. Albans. He knows the case, he's the best one to advise on new exercises. The last thing we want to do is tear open something that's already on the point of healing. And an X-ray might well be in order. I don't have access to a machine, I'm afraid."

Peter, dressed again, made a face as he came out of the doctor's surgery. "Did he tell you? Back to St. Albans. I'd rather go back to Aldshot."

"Yes, I'm sure, but the thing is, we must do what's best." I couldn't help but think that if I made it possible for Peter to heal, he'd be back in the thick of the fighting again. And I couldn't bear to contemplate that. The next time he was wounded . . .

"St. Albans it is," he said with a sigh.

And so we went on to St. Albans, stopping briefly in London for a late meal. The doctors at the clinic were pleased to see him, and Dr. Fuller said, "You've clearly been in good hands, Captain. I'm impressed with the progress you've made. Still a way to go, of course, but your general health has improved."

It had. He had regained the weight he'd lost, and except for stiffness in his arm, looked fit and remarkably handsome.

Peter glanced at me, and I could almost read what was passing through his mind—*happiness made all the difference.* Aloud, he said, "I've walked every day, and my appetite has picked up."

"Yes, and I dare say a good night's rest hasn't gone amiss. We'd like to keep you a day or so, to see how the arm responds and to teach you the new exercises. Will that be all right with your chauffeur?" He turned to smile at me.

"I'd like to run down to London and look in on Mrs. Hennessey," I said to Peter. "It should work out well."

I could see in the tightness around his mouth how sad he was that our idyll was over.

We said good-bye shortly afterward, and I went on to the inn where I'd stayed before. Early the next morning, rather than interrupt the schedule at the clinic, I drove on to London without seeing Peter.

Mrs. Hennessey, on her way home from marketing, saw me arrive and said in a fluster, "My dear! I just posted a letter to you in Sussex yesterday morning. And here you are!"

"A letter? From whom?" There had been no letters for either of us in Aldshot.

"From France, Elspeth. I knew you'd be eager to get it. And then this morning there was something from Queen

Alexandra's Imperial Military Nursing Service. I put it in the post just now."

The official notification of my resignation. It could wait. But the letter from France . . .

Peter would be in St. Albans for another day. I could easily drive back to Sussex, find my letter, and return before he was discharged.

It was silly to make such a long circuit, but if there was bad news, the sooner I knew the better.

I thanked Mrs. Hennessey, reversed the motorcar, and set out for Sussex.

It was late when I reached the cottage. There had been a military convoy on the road and an overturned caisson. It had held me up for an hour or more.

I let myself in and fumbled for the lamp, lighting it and looking at the fire. Mrs. Wright, bless her, had kept it up, and the room was comfortably warm.

My ring lay where I'd left it, on the mantel shelf. I picked it up, slipped it over my finger again, and then in a spasm of guilt, took it off and put it back on the shelf once more.

Mrs. Wright came hurrying over, apologizing for not having my dinner ready. "But we weren't sure how long you might be in Midhurst, and I kept it warm in my kitchen instead. I'll have it quick as a wink." She looked around. "Where's the Captain? Has he gone up to lie down?"

"He's in St. Albans. The doctor wanted to keep him for several days. I came back because I'm expecting a letter to arrive."

"There's been no post this last day or so. I expect everyone is still busy with Christmas and all. Sit down and warm yourself by the fire. I'll come back shortly."

She started out the door, but I got up and hurried after her.

"Perhaps I could eat my dinner where I have my breakfast," I suggested. "And then go up to bed."

I couldn't sit here in the empty cottage any longer. I missed Peter's presence terribly.

"Well, if you like," she said, giving me a quick look. "The cottage does seem rather quiet without the Captain moving about. He's such a lovely man, the Captain. I don't know when I've met anyone finer. Come along, then. I'll step over and see to the fires later."

I ate my dinner alone, and then went up to bed. I tried to read a little in one of the books I'd been reading to Peter, but in the end, I fell asleep, letting it slide to the floor with a thump.

The next morning I waited for the post to arrive. It hadn't come by eleven, its usual time, and I told myself that there was nothing for Aldshot, that I'd have to wait until tomorrow for my letter.

And then close on to two o'clock, there was a knock at the door, and I hurried to answer it. There was the post van, and a man muffled to the eyes in a new scarf, clearly a Christmas gift from someone in the family—I could see the dropped stitches and where a different shade of blue had been employed halfway through—held out a letter to me.

"I'd thought of not coming at all," he said, "since this was the only letter for Aldshot, but it was foreign like, and I thought it might be . . . news."

He'd nearly said *bad news*.

I thanked him and hurried back inside, to sit by the fire as I opened the envelope.

The letter was from Madeleine.

> *You must come at once. They've exchanged Alain for one of their own, and he's in Paris, with me. He's in terrible straits, and I don't know what to do. Please find a way to come. I beg of you.*

That was all. But it was enough.

I sat there, reading it over again, trying to think what Madeleine had meant by "terrible straits."

And then I jumped up, realizing that I must go.

But there was Peter, what was I to do about Peter? He was so much stronger, so much better, he had come so far . . .

He would need the motorcar. He wasn't ready to take the train. I couldn't leave without making certain Peter was all right.

I crossed to the Wrights' house, went upstairs and

packed my valise, then went in search of Mrs. Wright. She was out in the back garden, feeding the hens, and she looked up as I called to her.

"What's wrong? Is anything wrong?" she asked, seeing my face.

"A friend is in trouble. I must go," I said. "I'm so sorry, Mrs. Wright, but it's urgent. I'll drive back to London and leave the motorcar there for the Captain. If I don't—tell him—tell him I'll write as soon as I can." I couldn't go on.

Our extraordinary interlude at Walnut Tree Cottage had come to an end.

I thought my heart would break.

And then I was out in the motorcar, turning to go back to Midhurst, where I could pick up the road to London.

The morning had been dull, but as I was reversing, a ray of sunlight came through the clouds, bathing the walnut tree in light.

I stopped, got out, and ran into the front garden, finding a walnut for Sister Blake. I didn't know when I'd see her, but it would do no harm to have it with me, ready to pay our "rent." And then I was gone.

I was halfway to London when I remembered the other letter that Mrs. Hennessey had posted to me. It could wait. I needed no official letter to tell me what I had lost.

Once in London I drove directly to Mrs. Hennessey's house.

Bess was in residence, having been given a week's leave.

She was just on her way to Victoria Station to take the train to Somerset. I stopped her and begged a favor.

"I know you are eager to see your family," I began, "but I need your help desperately."

"What's wrong? What do you need?" she asked instantly, ready to help.

I explained about France, and how I must reach Paris as soon as possible.

Why Peter was in St. Albans and must return to Sussex.

She listened, then nodded. "It will be all right, I'll drive to St. Albans and retrieve your Peter, then take him to Sussex. What shall I tell him? He'll want to know why you're deserting him."

"Tell him—just tell him I was called away. And, Bess, could I borrow one of your uniforms? I'll return it to you as soon as possible."

"Yes, of course, they're in my wardrobe in the flat. But where are yours?"

"It's a long story. For another day. Hurry, Peter will be waiting." And I dashed into the house and up the stairs, leaving her with her kit and Peter's motorcar.

I changed quickly. It was against all rules to wear this uniform without proper sanction. But I couldn't imagine that I would be allowed to travel to France as a civilian. A nursing Sister returning to her post would stand a fairly good chance.

I had a little trouble getting a ticket for Dover. Once there I found a ship's officer I knew and told him that I had missed my connection because my train was delayed. He agreed to land me in Calais. "I don't have a cabin for you," he ended, in apology.

"It doesn't matter. I'll be fine." I thanked heaven he hadn't asked for my orders, assuming I had them.

The crossing was winter rough, and I sat on deck, watching the waves crashing over the bow. A good many of the new recruits were seasick, lying on deck where it was cooler than the stuffy quarters below or hanging over the rail, moaning in agony and praying for the ship's corkscrew motion to stop.

I shut them out of my mind, wondering how I would manage to reach Paris once I was in France. But that turned out to be no problem. I found a convoy of lorries on their way to Rouen, and once in Rouen, I took the first train in any direction. It was heading south, but it didn't matter, for I was able to pick up another going on to Paris once I'd reached Lyon.

It was interesting to see that my uniform—Bess's—a few well-placed lies or sous, and the reputation of the Nursing Service got me through, where once orders had been paramount. I was grateful for the changes time had brought.

In Paris I found a taxi to take me to the Villard house, and finally, tired, travel stained, worried almost to the point of feeling ill, I was lifting the Villard's massive knocker and waiting for someone to answer my summons.

It was Marie, Madeleines's maid, who came to the door. She exclaimed when she recognized me and ushered me inside. At that moment, Madeleine herself came rushing down the stairs, her face alight with surprise and relief.

"Elspeth? Is that you? Of course it is! Come in, Marie will make tea for you while you warm yourself by the fire." She enveloped me in a loving embrace, then linking her arm with mine, she led me into the little morning room where she wrote her letters and dealt with household accounts.

"We seldom light the fires in the drawing room," she said, pulling up a chair for me. "Coal and wood are hard to come by, and we make do as best we can. Oh, this is the first time I've seen you in your uniform. Turn around and let me—yes, very nice, but it isn't you, is it, Elspeth, my dear?"

"It was this uniform that brought me across England and then over half of France, to you," I told her. "A ball gown or an evening gown wouldn't have worked at all."

And then I regretted my sharpness. How was Madeleine to know how much my nursing had meant to me? But she laughed, thinking I was teasing.

"Tell me—your letter just reached me a few days ago, and you said in it that Alain had been exchanged?"

"We had an officer they wanted rather badly. Henri managed to include Alain in the price for him. And just as well. He's been so terribly ill, Elspeth, so changed, in such despair."

"What happened? You said he'd been wounded when he was captured, but no one seemed to know where or how seriously."

"They had to take his arm, Elspeth. At the shoulder. It was that or let him die of gangrene." She began to cry, the pent-up emotions of Alain's return and his condition too much to hold in any longer. "His *arm*, Elspeth. I can't bear it."

I had seen more amputations than she could imagine in her wildest dreams. But this was Alain. Her brother, the man I'd thought I wanted to marry when he marched off to war.

And then I realized the full impact of his amputation. I could hardly tell him now that I'd fallen in love with someone else. Not now, not ever.

"I want to see him. Will you take me up to his room?"

"Have your tea first, Elspeth. You'll need all your strength to face what's ahead."

I could have told her I needed nothing but to see Alain for myself. Still, I was a guest in her house, and she had ordered the tea especially on my account.

And so I sat there and drank my tea, ate the little cakes that the Villard cook had added to the tea tray, and listened to the rest of Madeleine's news.

Little Henri was growing, just learning to crawl. Henri was no longer with the British forces as liaison but back with his old regiment.

"I worry about him every day, pray for him every night. He came home with Alain, twenty-four hours, that's all he had. But he saw his son, I held him in my arms, and that was that. He was gone away again almost as soon as he'd come."

I was glad for both their sakes that they'd had even that little time together.

"And he says—he says that the war that was to end by

Christmas will go on and on and on. There's no way of knowing how or when it will end." She was crying again. "What will I do if something happens to Henri? Bad enough that Alain is like he is. But my God, what if it had been Henri?"

I comforted her as best I could and finally persuaded her to take me upstairs to see Alain. At the door of his bedchamber, she stopped.

"Go and see him, Elspeth. Let me wait here for you."

It was then I realized that she had been putting off seeing him because she herself dreaded going into his room.

I braced myself for a shock, knocked lightly, and when Alain's familiar voice called gruffly, "Come," I opened the door and walked into his bedroom.

He was sitting by the fire. So thin that I hardly knew him, his fair hair cropped short as a result of his fever, and his face drawn with pain and despair.

He recognized me at once, and I saw from his expression that Madeleine hadn't told him that she'd written to me.

It was his right arm that was missing, the shoulder of his shirt sagging where it had been.

Trying to rise to his feet, he nearly fell, and swore with feeling under his breath.

"Elspeth," he said. And that was all he could manage.

"Alain. My dear," I said, crossing the room to the hearth and holding out my hands to the blaze. I wanted so much to take him into my arms and comfort him, but he would have seen that as pity. And pity he didn't want from me. "It was a cold journey. I'm glad to be here. How are you?"

"As you see," he said bitterly.

"Yes, you've been through a terrible ordeal. How is the shoulder?"

Shocked that I should ask, he couldn't answer at first. Then he said, "I feel the arm. Every day. Every night I dream that I'm whole. And every morning I wake up to find that it's not there."

"It's not uncommon," I said slowly. "It could fade with time. There's no way of knowing."

"I asked Madeleine not to tell you," he burst out angrily. "I forbade her to write to you. But I see that she has. I shan't be able to forgive her."

I turned to face him. "Did you think I wouldn't wish to know? I'd been told that you were missing, that you were taken prisoner, that you were wounded and very ill. Did you think I wouldn't care?"

He had the grace to look away. And then he turned back to me and said, "You aren't wearing my ring."

I lifted my hand and pulled the chain free of my collar, letting the light play on the gold and the ruby stone. It looked like fresh blood.

"I was not allowed to wear such things as a nursing Sister."

"Yes, I'd heard that you had trained. I admire your courage."

It was the first kind thing he'd said to me. "Thank you. My cousin Kenneth didn't see it that way at all. He insisted that I resign."

"And did you?"

"That's another story," I said evasively. "Will you ask me to sit down? Or shall I remain standing, like you?"

He gestured to a chair across from his, and once I had seated myself, he took the other, but awkwardly, his body not yet accustomed to balancing without that right arm.

We sat in silence for several minutes.

Then Alain said, "In a way I'm glad you've come. I have been trying to think how to tell you that I will not be speaking to your cousin after all."

I tried not to show my shock. "Your feelings toward me have changed?"

"Nothing has changed, Elspeth. Except for this." He indicated his shoulder. "I can't very well expect you to marry a wreck of the man you knew before the war began."

"Why should that make any difference? I've seen terrible things in the aid stations where I've served. Losing an arm is not the worst of them."

"Don't make light of what I've been through," he said angrily. "And don't tell me that I don't know what I'm saying."

I was thinking that it could just as easily have been Peter who had lost his arm, not Alain. God had chosen. And I must make my choice. Clearly. Now.

"I'm not making light of anything. If you don't care for me any longer, I can understand that and I can learn to accept it. What you are doing instead is denying me the right to choose. And I won't allow you to take that from me, Alain. I told you before you left to join your regiment that I was pleased that you were intending to speak to Cousin

Kenneth when the war was at an end. Well, it has ended for you. I can carry a letter to Scotland. It will be some time before you can travel, and Cousin Kenneth will take that into account."

"I'm not marrying you or any woman. Not now, not ever."

"There are other offers for my hand. Will you let him decide to accept one of them instead?"

"I have no choice." There was anguish in his voice.

"Then you don't love me, do you? I'm sorry." It was merciless—but it was the only way to break through his stubborn resistance. I didn't know if it would do more harm than good in the end, but I had come all this way to find him again, and I refused to be turned away.

I stood up, preparing to leave the room.

"For God's sake, Elspeth, think what you're doing to me."

"No. It is what you are doing to me, Alain. Let's be clear about this."

He stood up, anger in his eyes, his jaw taut. "All right. If you want to know, I love you still. As much as I did in August. More, because I've thought about you every day in that wretched prison. You were the brightness in my darkness, and I think the only reason I survived at all was because of you. But that's a two-edged sword, Elspeth. I have loved you too much. And I should have died. I should never have lived through that surgery."

I wanted desperately to go to him, hold him. And I dared not.

"Do you think I only loved you when you were whole?" I asked. "Alain, do you think I'm so shallow?"

He stared at me. "My dear girl. I'm not what I was!"

"You are still Alain, aren't you? Write that letter, and I will take it to Scotland in your place."

"I can't—"

"You can."

I turned away, hiding the tears in my eyes. "I'm very tired, it was a long journey and I wasn't able to sleep very much. I'd like to lie down. When I'm rested, I'll come back. Don't shut me out, Alain. Please."

And with that I left the room.

Madeleine was still outside the door.

"I heard you shouting at each other," she said uneasily.

"Yes. But in the end, I think I got my way."

She embraced me then, holding me fiercely. "You'll still be my sister, won't you? And we'll be just like we were before, the four of us, happy together."

"If only we could," I said, against her fair hair.

And meant it.

• *Chapter Twelve* •

WHEN NEXT I SAW ALAIN, he was in a very different mood. I told myself that my bluntness had brought him to his senses. He began to talk about the weeks before the war, about his sister's schooling at the Académie, about his life growing up at Montigny.

But never about the fighting he had seen along the Marne.

Over the next week, we settled into a comfortable way of going on.

One afternoon Alain talked about seeing me for the first time. He had come to escort his sister home for the Christmas holidays, and I had been in the foyer of the school as he walked in.

"You were frowning," he said. "An absolute thundercloud. I asked Madeleine later what it was that troubled you, and she told me that you hadn't wanted to leave England to finish your education. That you had lost your father and it had been very painful because it was so sudden, so unexpected."

"That's true," I said, remembering. "It seemed that I'd lost everything. My father, my home, my country. Cousin Kenneth is a very good man, he tries to carry out my father's wishes in every way. But sometimes he's dreadfully inflexible."

"As in forcing you to leave the Nursing Service."

I regarded him for a moment. "Would you refuse to consider marrying me because I had been a nursing Sister in the war?"

"I was a soldier," he said very simply. "I knew your worth. To men in pain, men dying, you were sisters of mercy. I would not have felt that this changed you in any way."

He had used the past tense. I was wearing his ring now. He had commented on it. And I had changed into the clothing I had worn here before the war began, left in the wardrobe of my room, cleaned and pressed with loving care by Madeleine's maid.

I had come here to find him again. To see if the man he had been was changed in any way. Save for that first night, he had become the Alain I knew, his anger gone.

But now the use of the past tense worried me. I didn't know how to probe for his feelings, for one could hardly ask a onetime suitor if he still wished to marry one.

Suddenly I was reminded of a story about Queen Victoria, that she had had to propose marriage to Prince Albert, for she as a reigning queen could not be offered marriage in the usual way.

Well, wasn't I an Earl's daughter? And for all his blue blood, Alain Montigny could be considered a commoner, without a title . . .

I said, "I have another question. You can't travel to Scotland—Cousin Kenneth can't come to Paris. At least, not very easily in the middle of a war. But the post still carries letters to and from Scotland. I don't think it would be very proper for me to write to Cousin Kenneth on your behalf. But perhaps there is someone you could ask. A priest, a solicitor. I don't want to lose you a second time."

He looked away. "It's too early, Elspeth. I have hardly healed. I can't rise from a chair without risking a fall. I must see my doctor every week. I haven't yet learned to use my left hand properly. I'm not prepared to be a bridegroom."

He hadn't talked to me about the war. And he hadn't touched my hand or even kissed me on the cheek—as he had done when I was no more than Madeleine's Scots friend.

"One doesn't have to marry straightaway. A long betrothal is not unexpected in wartime."

Alain turned back to me. "You must understand, my dear." He lifted his left hand to touch the sleeve of his missing arm. "I must learn how to live with it. Not to be morbid, but I wake at night, and I've dreamed the arm was still there. I was back in the Marne Valley, sending my men out of harm's way, taking over that German machine gun and turning it around on the soldiers coming toward me. Or I'm being forced to march back behind the German lines, my arm bleeding but still there. I won't bore you with the rest, but you will understand. And you as a Scot might understand this as well. Without an arm, I can't go back and fight them again and take my revenge for the care given me that cost me my arm."

I was shocked. I *hadn't* understood. I'd been ready to go forward with our official engagement, it was one of the reasons I had hurried to France. I understood duty, I understood responsibility and honor and pride. But not what Alain had endured.

Or that it would become more important in his life than anything—or anyone—else.

"I'm glad you confided in me," I told him with bald honesty.

He smiled. "That's one of the reasons I love you, Elspeth. One of many."

And he changed the subject.

As we talked about young Henri, I realized I hadn't yet touched Alain, just as he had not touched me.

Was I afraid to? Afraid of his reaction to it? Or was it Peter, and my feelings for him?

Truth was, I didn't know.

A second week passed. I persuaded Alain to walk with me as I pushed little Henri's pram down the street, trailed by his anxious nurse. Alain was clearly unhappy to be in such a public place, where his pinned sleeve drew attention. He wasn't the only veteran on the street. I saw men with crutches and empty sleeves, disfigured faces and bound eyes, missing ears, hands, feet. But Alain was still a very attractive man, and that drew attention too. We must have seemed like a very happy pair, taking our child for a stroll.

But it didn't last long. He said tightly, "I must go back. I'm . . . tired."

I didn't argue. I turned the pram, and we walked quickly back to the Villard house. And Alain didn't come down to dinner.

I tried to talk to Madeleine about Alain, but she was blind to what I saw. I wished Henri were here, or one of my cousins, someone I could confide in. I even considered going to see his doctor, but I knew I wouldn't be told anything of importance—I wasn't a wife, not even officially betrothed. And I was a woman, after all, to be spared "unpleasantness."

Worried, I wrote to Bess Crawford in England, praying that she was there and not in France. I asked her to speak to her father. He had been a regimental Colonel, he had had experience in handling men who were in battle and had been wounded. I hoped he could guide me in what I could do to help Alain.

And at the same time I took hope from one thing. While Alain had done nothing to resume the closeness between us of that night before he left to join his regiment, he had not sent me away. Or asked me to return his mother's ring.

It was a beginning.

I had to be satisfied with that. And Peter? That door

must remain closed. Forever. It was cowardly of me not to tell Peter about Alain. I think he guessed when I never wore his Christmas ring that there was a reason. But he too had tried to pretend we had a future together. Two blind lovers under the spell of a walnut tree . . .

There was to be no happy ending for us.

The next week went surprisingly well, after the debacle of the walk with the pram. Alain was even affectionate. And the week after that, one night he kissed me on the cheek before I went up to my room to bed. It was a brotherly kiss, the sort he would give his sister, yet I thought it lingered a little longer than a brother's kiss might have done.

On Thursday, he kissed me on the lips. But there was no passion in that kiss either. More longing, I thought, and sadness.

Friday morning Alain left in the motorcar, the Villard chauffeur driving—an elderly man who had been sent for from the family estates in the Loire Valley. I wished him well, for he was reporting to the surgeon who had seen to his care since his return to Paris. I willed the doctor to tell Alain that he was recovering remarkably well.

"There will be good news, I hope. I've seen such improvement, myself." I smiled. "We'll have something to celebrate."

He held my hand for a moment, then said, "My love."

Madeleine and I took young Henri for his daily walk, although it was very cold that morning and we were wearing our warmest coats. A small fur coverlet kept the baby warm. He was waving mittened fists in the air, and Madeleine was watching him with adoration in her eyes.

"He's growing more like his father every day, don't you think?" she asked.

"Absolutely," I answered, smiling.

"Wait until you have your own," she told me happily. "You can't imagine what it's like. A part of you, a part of Alain, together in one little child."

She had just received a brief letter from Henri, and her joy was contagious.

And I very much wanted to believe in her rosy prediction. It would surely be Alain's salvation. And perhaps mine as well.

We returned to the house, and by the time we had changed out of our walking dresses, I had quite an appetite. Food was not plentiful, but the Villard cook was a genius at making whatever he could find into a tasty dish.

Walking into the chilly dining room, I found Madeleine already there. She nodded to the maid to begin serving. "Marie has just told me that Alain hasn't returned from his appointment with Dr. Lorville. He's the surgeon. I hope this doesn't mean more surgery. I don't think I could bear it."

"The wound is healing. I can't believe there is any need for more surgery. I expect it's the growing number of patients. More wounded appear to be coming into Paris every day, many of them in dire need of further care."

But she wasn't convinced. Her concern for her brother was second only to her worry about Henri, and it was a constant anxiety, never far from her thoughts.

I finished my soup and the plate was taken away. Madeleine lingered over hers, listening for the sound of Alain's uneven footsteps coming down the passage.

We were eating our cheese when Madeleine was called away. Alain's driver had just pulled into the courtyard in front of the house. And Alain was not in the carriage.

"He's been taken directly to hospital," she exclaimed as she rose and flew down the passage, leaving Marie standing there. "It's infection. They warned me of infection. How dangerous it could be."

"What is it, Marie? Do you know?" I asked as I hurried after Madeleine.

"No, my lady—"

They were in the foyer, Madeleine and Arnaud, the driver.

She was bombarding him with questions, and he stood there, his eyes frightened, his mouth open, not knowing which to answer first.

When she burst into tears, I managed to ask, "Arnaud. Where is Monsieur? Is he in hospital?"

"No, my lady." He bobbed his head in what passed for a bow, and then went on in rapid French, "We left the doctor's after one hour, my lady, and Monsieur asked if I would drive him to the Bois, that he felt like a little fresh air after the stuffy surgery. It was a fine day, *vous comprenez,* even though a little cold. I thought nothing of it. We drove for a time, and then he asked me to stop and wait awhile for him. He said that you, my lady, and the doctor had encouraged him to walk, and he thought he would practice a little now. I did as I was told, my lady. But he did not return. I came here, not knowing what I must do. I fear he has met with—"

Madeleine interrupted, her voice shrill with anger now. "He could have fallen, did you not think of that? If he fell, he couldn't get up again."

"If he fell, Madame, he would have called out to me. I listened, but I heard nothing."

"Then you're deaf," she cried. Turning to me, she begged, "We must go back with him and look for Alain. If he's hurt, I shall send this man back to Villard and find myself a driver who is capable of doing his duty. It's so cold—Alain will have taken a chill, lying on the ground, and it will make him ill. We must take blankets, a hot water bottle—"

"That will take too long. Wait here, Madeleine, someone could have found him and is already bringing him to the house. Or if they carry him to hospital, someone will send word. I'll go with Arnaud. If Alain has injured his shoulder, I'll take him directly to the surgeon and send Arnaud back to tell you." I turned and lifting my skirts, I flew up the stairs, ignoring her protests.

Collecting a hat, my coat and my gloves, I came down again to find Madeleine had followed the old man out to the carriage and was still berating him. He seemed to shrink into himself as she accused him of selfishness, of thinking only of his midday meal, of leaving her brother to die.

I said hastily, "You must go inside, Madeleine, or you will take a chill yourself. Marie—" Pushing Arnaud toward the box, I managed to open the door of the carriage and let down the step, wishing the old man could manage a motorcar. I thought for a moment that Madeleine was going to insist on coming with us, but then she turned away, letting Marie shut the door at last.

Arnaud said over his shoulder as he lifted the reins and signaled the horses to walk on, "I have done nothing wrong, my lady. I waited as he asked. But he was gone so long. I walked a little way myself, and I called his name, but there was no answer."

I wondered if Arnaud was, in fact, a little deaf. Usually it was the higher ranges that older people lost first, but it was possible that Arnaud had reached a point where he could hear what was said to him directly but not at any distance.

Threading our way through the midday traffic, we finally reached the Bois on the outskirts of Paris. My own anxiety was growing with every mile as I considered all the possibilities. Finally Arnaud pulled up into a small clearing and said, "It was here I waited. You will see just there the cigarettes I smoked while waiting."

Those strong, smelly French cigarettes. I could pick out half a dozen stubs.

He helped me down. Looking around, I said, "Which direction, Arnaud? There, through the trees, or over there, along the bridle path."

"Toward the trees, my lady. He had forgot his cane, it was in the doctor's surgery. He thought he might find a stick there."

I began walking in that direction.

Twenty yards away, well within hearing distance, I called Arnaud's name. He was checking the harness on the horses. I called again, and he didn't turn.

I kept walking, but now I was calling Alain's name. Madeleine was right, it wouldn't do for him to be out in this cold for very long. I hadn't thought to see if he had taken his powders with him to his appointment. If he had, then if he was in great pain, he could take one. But that would make him drowsy, not alert enough, perhaps, to hear me call.

I came out of the trees into another small clearing. And as soon as I did, I saw him lying there.

"Alain!" I cried, and rushed toward him, nearly tripping on an exposed root. Was that what he'd done? Had he fallen and injured that shoulder beyond bearing, losing consciousness?

I knelt beside him. He was lying on his good shoulder, his face turned away. Certain he had fainted, I gently pulled him over on his back, into my arms, saying as I did, "My dear, I've come, I'm here, we'll have you home and in bed—"

And as I gathered him close, to warm him a little, his face turning toward me, I saw for the first time the small round hole in his temple, the dark trickle of blood down his cheek, soaking into the cloth of his coat.

And beneath him, half hidden by his left hand, lay his service revolver.

• *Chapter Thirteen* •

I REMEMBER CRYING OUT, TOO shocked to think, and then my training took over. Stripping off my gloves, I felt frantically for a pulse, hoping against impossible hope that I would feel the thread of his heartbeat.

But there was none, and his body was already cooling, the warmth that was Alain slipping away here on the half frozen ground.

And still I sat there, cradling him in my arms, unable to cry.

There was Madeleine, waiting anxiously.

I got to my feet, saw that I had his blood on my hands, and stared at them for what seemed like hours but was only a matter of seconds. All I could think of was that Alain's blood was darker than the ruby on my finger.

I stumbled back the way I'd come, to see Arnaud standing patiently by his horses, just as he had done before while Alain brought the revolver up to his temple.

He hadn't heard the shot. He hadn't known, when he

was waiting for Monsieur to return, that Alain Montigny was already dead.

What in God's name am I to tell Madeleine? The thought was like a blow.

When I was close enough for the old man to hear me, I called to him. "You must turn the horses. We shall have to find another way through the trees to a small clearing. Monsieur is there."

He helped me into the carriage and then did as I asked, but it took us a quarter of an hour to find our way through a tangle of undergrowth to where Alain lay.

By that time I'd told Arnaud that Monsieur was dead.

We collected his body and between us laid it gently in the carriage.

I picked up the service revolver, thrust it under the carriage robe that covered Alain, and told Arnaud to return to the Villard house.

Sitting there in the carriage beside his body, I tried to make sense of what Alain had done.

That was when I decided to carry Alain back to Dr. Lorville's surgery, not to the house. For one thing it would be better for Madeleine. For another I wanted to know what the doctor had told him during his examination.

As the horses trotted along the hard packed earth of the forest track and finally reached the cobblestone streets of the city, turning toward the doctor's surgery, my shock and horror gave way to a numbness that was a blessing. For I would have to be strong for Madeleine. There was no one else.

When Arnaud pulled up by the door, I got down, walked into the doctor's crowded reception room, and said to the young woman sitting there, "I have Monsieur Montigny in the carriage outside. It's urgent that I speak to the doctor at once."

"He has just finished with a patient, Mademoiselle. Is there something I can do for you? Has Monsieur taken ill? Or hurt himself?"

"Please. I must see the doctor."

She nodded, and after a five-minute wait that felt like an eternity I was shown into the inner officer where Dr. Lorville spoke to patients after his examinations.

"Mademoiselle?" He offered me a chair across from his desk. "Are you the sister of Monsieur Montigny? I understood that she was married?"

"I'm a close friend of the family. I am here on Madame Villard's behalf. Today did you lead Monsieur Montigny to believe that more surgery was imminent?"

"On the contrary, I told him that his wound and the site of the amputation had healed well, and that I saw no reason why he could not live a fairly normal life. I released him to the care of his own physician. Has he not told you this?"

"There was no—no bad news?"

"Not at all, Mademoiselle. I was quite pleased that he was well enough to get on with his life," he said again, a touch of impatience in his voice.

I said without softening the blow, "Monsieur Montigny left your surgery this morning and asked his driver to take him to the Bois, where he wished to walk a little. The driver is old and deaf. He didn't know where Monsieur went or why. But growing anxious, he searched a little and then came to the Villard house to tell us that he couldn't find Monsieur. I went back to the Bois with him—and I did find him. He had taken his service revolver with him and at some distance from the main road, he had shot himself."

As I recounted what had happened, I watched the growing alarm on the doctor's face as he realized why I had come to him.

Rising from his chair, he said, "Where is he? Still in the Bois?"

"I couldn't leave him there," I said, rising as well. "I couldn't take him to the Villard house. And so I brought him to you."

"Yes, quite right. I'll make the necessary arrangements. The undertakers . . ." He cleared his throat. "An accident with his revolver while practicing with his other hand. Yes, that will do."

He ushered me out of the office, following me outside to where the carriage waited.

Arnaud was sitting in the box, a statue in a blue uniform, staring straight ahead, as if refusing to acknowledge what lay in the carriage just behind him.

He turned as we came out of the surgery and watched as the doctor confirmed what I had known from the moment I had knelt beside Alain and gathered him into my arms.

"Yes. Dead. I will have him carried into the surgery through the side door there. I'll sign the death certificate.

And I will summon the undertakers. Is there anything more that I can do? I would go to Madame Villard myself, but you can see, my surgery is full. But I advise you to send for her own physician."

"Madame Villard shouldn't be alone at such a time as this. Could you—would it be possible to arrange for compassionate leave for her husband, Major Villard?"

"I shall see to it. The Captain was quite a hero on the Marne. The Army will appreciate the need for a proper funeral."

I waited in the cold while an orderly was summoned. Alain's body, still covered by the carriage rug with the coat of arms of the Villard family in its center, was carried inside through the private entrance to the surgery.

Dr. Lorville said, "And you, Mademoiselle? Will you be all right? This has been a great shock."

"I was a battlefield nurse for the British Army," I said. "I have seen death before."

"But not," he said, considering me, "that of someone close to you."

"I have seen that too. But thank you for your concern."

He wasn't satisfied, but he nodded, then helped me into the carriage.

I spoke to Arnaud, and he turned the horses, taking me back to the Villard house.

I looked away from the seat beside me where Alain's body had lain, instead staring out the window and concentrating on how best to break such news to my friend. At least I wouldn't have to tell her Alain was a suicide. Mercifully, Dr. Lorville had seen to that. She would be spared gossip and speculation.

Between us, Marie and I got Madeleine upstairs and into her bed after she collapsed.

I went to Alain's room, thinking to find laudanum, hoping to give Madeleine a drop or two in warm milk, to allow her to sleep until her own doctor arrived.

There had been no time for me to mourn. But I could hear, over and over again, what the doctor had said, the words running through my mind like a chorus ever since Arnaud had driven me away from the surgery.

. . . released him . . . a normal life . . .

Then why had Alain chosen to die?

I found the laudanum in his dressing room. It wasn't until I was walking back through his bedroom that I saw the small envelope lying at the base of the gilt carriage clock that stood in the middle of the mantel shelf above the hearth.

I expected it to be addressed to Madeleine.

I was so afraid when I lifted it to look at Alain's elegant writing on the front that it might be addressed to me.

But it was not. Henri's name was there in black ink.

I stood there debating whether I should go ahead and open it. In the end, I left it where it was and took the laudanum back to Madeleine.

It was late the next afternoon when Henri walked through the door of his house, climbed the stairs without even stopping to remove his cap and greatcoat, and went directly to his wife's room.

I was sitting with her at the time, and I don't think I will ever forget the look on her face as her husband came toward her, his arms outstretched.

And then she was sobbing on his shoulder as if her heart would break, and I slipped quietly out and into the passage, closing the door gently behind me.

Henri came to find me later. I was sitting in the small morning room where the fire burned cheerfully on the hearth, but my hands felt as cold as death.

He had removed his hat and coat, and his uniform showed the rigors of travel, dusty and unpressed.

"They sent for me straightaway. I thought at first it must be Madeleine . . . or my son. I never dreamed it would be Alain." He was pacing up and down in front of the fire, unable to settle. "What happened? Do you know? She couldn't tell me, it was too difficult. Some nonsense about Alain practicing to fire his revolver with his left hand."

I gave him an account of finding Alain's body and taking him to Dr. Lorville's surgery, then said, "There's an envelope on the mantel shelf in his room. I saw it when I went to find laudanum for Madeleine. It's addressed to you."

He stopped in midstride. "Is there indeed!"

And then he was gone, out the door, his boots ringing on the stairs. Ten minutes later, he came back, the letter in his hand.

"What is it? Please, you must tell me."

His voice was husky as he spoke. "He has given me

certain information, such as where his will can be found and what he wishes to be done with his body. He asked me to beg Madeleine's pardon for his lack of courage. And he asked me to tell you that he loved you too much to tie you to half a man. But that he wished for you to keep his ring, in remembrance of him. He hopes you will be happy, think of him kindly, and understand why he had to make the decision to end his life."

"Then he knew—he knew, before he kept the appointment with the doctor."

"Yes. I imagine it was the only way to leave the house without arousing suspicion." Henri shook his head. "The fool. *The bloody damned fool.*"

And for an instant I thought he would ball up Alain's letter and hurl it into the fire.

Instead he set it carefully on the table, then walked to the cabinet against the wall, took out a glass and a decanter, and poured himself a brandy. Turning, he saw the grief I couldn't conceal, and said, "My dear, you need one as much as I do. You were to marry him. I would give anything—*anything*—to have spared you finding his body." He poured a small measure into another glass and brought it to me.

I drank it in one swallow, coughed a little, and then set the glass aside as the brandy warmed me a little. "I thought my being here would make a difference. I thought that if I let Alain know that nothing had changed, that I wanted to marry him whatever had happened, he would have a reason for living. But what I have done," I went on, my voice breaking, "what I have done is make him see all too clearly how bleak his future would be, that he couldn't go on. If I hadn't come, Alain would still be alive. He would have had no reason to kill himself, because he could live in this house as long as he liked, and never have to face what had been done to him by the war. He would have been safe, he could have come to terms with his lost arm in time, and found some measure of peace. Don't you see? It's all my fault."

For the first and only time since I had known Henri Villard, he took me in his arms, held me tightly for a moment, then moving his hands to my shoulders, he shook me.

"You're wrong, Elspeth. Wrong, do you hear me? Alain killed himself because he was in despair. He wrote to me soon after he arrived in Paris, after the first surgery. He told me that he wanted nothing more in life than to see you again. He got his wish. And after that, what was there to live for, in his mind?"

I hadn't known about that letter. Still, it was hurtful that I had come to Paris to be with him, and still I couldn't save him. I loved Alain. I had learned over these past weeks that I loved him in the same way I loved my cousin Bruce. Perhaps I had from the start, and confused it with more in the excitement of his going off to war. So long ago, it seemed another lifetime. I loved him enough that I would have given anything to save him. And I couldn't.

I don't think Alain ever guessed what I felt. I was so grateful for that. Even so, my sense of guilt was dreadful.

It was something I could never confess to Henri.

Henri let me go with a sigh.

"I must speak to the undertaker. Madeleine is sleeping at last, and they are expecting my visit."

"I don't know how she will go on," I replied. "But there is little Henri, he will be her anchor."

"Yes, but she will be changed forever. I can already see it. That lightness of heart, that intense feeling for those she loved, that need to have the rest of the world be happy with her. I remember the first time I saw her, she was like a lovely butterfly, touching everyone around her with happiness."

"You have changed as well," I said. "The war—"

"It has changed all of us. I don't know when it will end. Or how. But we will never go back to the innocence of our youth. That's over. A dream that we can barely remember."

His voice was so heavy with grief, for himself, for Madeleine, for Alain, that I wanted to cry. But he shrugged off the dark mood, put a comradely hand on my shoulder, and added, "Thank God you were here. That it wasn't Madeleine who found him. You saved my son, and now you have saved my wife. I will not forget."

He walked to the door without looking back and closed it behind him. I listened to his footsteps fading down the passage.

The funeral, I thought. How am I to get through the funeral, when all I can see is Alain's lifeless body in my arms, his fair hair stiff with drying blood, his blue eyes closed forever, and the warmth that was *Alain* slowly seeping away.

I would manage in some fashion.

I was an Earl's daughter, and I had been taught to conceal my feelings in public. I had already been tested, following behind my father's coffin.

Henri had arranged a military funeral, no whisper of suicide, and the cortege wound its way through the streets of Paris toward the columns and tall, mismatched towers of Saint-Sulpice. Alain had attended services there whenever he was in Paris, because of its magnificent organ. Henri had told me that Monsieur Widor himself would be playing for the service, for he had known Alain.

The coffin—Alain's coffin—was placed below the high altar, draped with the French flag, and on it lay his dress cap, his sword, and a cushion holding the medals he had been awarded. Sunlight coming through the high windows bathed it in soft light.

A hero.

Duty had taken him into the army, and duty had made him brave, and in the end, duty had killed him.

We three sat together, Henri in his dress uniform. Madeleine and I in black, heavy veils shielding our faces and hiding our tears. On my finger I still wore the ruby ring. The stone, usually such a rich deep red, seemed dull today.

Because of the war, the great church was nearly empty of mourners. There were those who knew the Villards, those who knew Alain, and men who had served with him, their uniforms bright splashes of color amongst the somber black of the civilians. The priest's voice and the hymns echoed around the stone walls, the notes of the organ soaring above our heads into the intricate ribbed vaulting of the nave. Henri delivered the eulogy, his voice firm, his words that of a soldier and a friend. It was a lovely service, but I heard very little of it, staring at the coffin and thinking of what might have been if there had been no war. I'd have married Alain, possibly in this church or in the chapel at Montigny. We would have lived together into contented old age, our children around us. I would never have met Peter Gilchrist again on the Calais-to-Ypres road . . .

My fault, for insisting on returning to England.

I've always known my own mind. Sometimes it's a curse.

And then the Mass was over, and we filed out of the church.

Alain was to be buried in Père-Lachaise Cemetery because Henri's leave was too short to allow the funeral cortege to make its way to Montigny in Burgundy.

I stood there watching the coffin being lowered into the winter-bare earth, added my bouquet of violets, hard to come by at this time of year, to the other flowers strewn gently over it, and then I winced as a company from his regiment fired their rifles over the grave in a final salute.

Afterward the three of us spoke quietly to everyone who had come, thanking them for their support in our grief. At length the condolences were at an end, and the three of us returned to the motorcar. Michel, the new chauffeur, was driving now, Arnaud having been pensioned off to

Villard. When we walked into the house, it seemed to echo our footsteps, emphasizing our loss and the fact that we would never see Alain here again. And yet Alain had lived here only a little while, and even then mostly in his suite of rooms.

Madeleine and I went up to remove our coats and hats, then walked back down the stairs together to the dining room, where a cold luncheon was served. The remaining staff had asked to attend the service, and so there was no hot meal.

It didn't matter, I could barely swallow what was set before me, and Madeleine after a bite or two, put down her fork.

"You must leave in three days' time?" she asked her husband, although she already knew the answer.

"I'm afraid so, my love."

She turned to me. "And you, Elspeth? You will leave now for England?"

"I will stay as long as you like, Madeleine."

She surprised me by answering, "I would rather you go. I'd hoped you would be my sister, but that's at an end. You now remind me too much of what I have lost. Alone, I can pretend, a little." She broke off, biting her lip. I saw the tears well in her eyes. "Please, Elspeth, do you understand? It will help me heal."

I was hurt, but I knew what she was asking and why. France was no longer my home.

"I shall need a pass to travel back to England," I said.

"Perhaps Henri will be able to arrange one for me."

"Consider it done," he said, but I could tell, seeing the frown between his eyes, that he was unhappy about his wife's decision. He had hoped, I thought, that I'd stay on at least until the period of mourning was over. Still, it was her choice to make, after all.

And perhaps I should leave Paris and my own memories here. Perhaps it was for the best . . .

Chapter Fourteen

Two days after Henri left Paris to rejoin his regiment, I set out for Rouen, this time with all my belongings carefully packed into a trunk and a valise.

Henri had obtained my pass, and he kissed me on the cheek when he said good-bye.

I had the strongest feeling that it would be a very long time before I saw him again, and I thought perhaps he had had the same premonition. Madeleine's grief went too deep to measure. I wouldn't be returning to Paris. I wished him well, told him that he must come home safe to Madeleine and his son.

He smiled, promised, and then was gone.

Madeleine had come down to see me off. Michel had brought the motorcar around—Henri insisted that I must not travel to Rouen by train. He had fretted that I didn't have a maid to accompany me. But I had traveled to Calais alone in the midst of the fighting and I felt no fear for my safety.

All the same I was grateful for his care.

I reached Rouen and discovered that Henri had sent word to the port authorities that I had been in Paris to attend the funeral of my fiancé, a hero of the Marne.

And so I was treated with every courtesy.

There was a ship sailing with the next tide. There was no cabin available, but I didn't care. I could hear the heavy guns in the north, a push on, and there was nothing I could do about the wounded, the dying that would soon be flooding the forward aid stations. Instead I stood by the rail and watched France fade slowly into the distance, remembering my school days in Paris, remembering sharing whispered confidences in the dark with Madeleine when we ought to have been sleeping, remembering watching from the upstairs window for Alain to arrive in the Montigny carriage to collect his sister. All in the past now. I felt an overwhelming sadness. Madeleine and Alain lost to me. My work as a Sister taken from me. Even the chatty artillery Captain, his ear and throat swathed in bandages, who came to stand beside me at the rail couldn't lighten my mood.

We had a rough crossing, and as always there was the fear of a German submarine lurking somewhere in the Channel. When the Isle of Wight appeared off the port bow, and then the entrance to the harbor at Portsmouth loomed just ahead, I thought I might feel as if I had come home.

But where was my home now?

Portsmouth was busy, crowded. I didn't want to stay the night there.

With the help of the stationmaster, I was able to find space on a train going to London, my luggage loaded in the van. I sat by the window, watching the lights of Hampshire villages flash by. Not terribly far from where I was traveling now, over the border into Sussex, was the tiny village of Aldshot. By now Peter would have gone back to St. Albans a second time for further treatment. After that, he should be released to live in his own flat until he was judged well enough to return to France.

I couldn't go to him. Not now. Not ever. It would be a betrayal of Alain in my heart. His suicide had made it impossible.

We pulled into London, and I sent my trunk to Cousin Kenneth's house to be stored for the time being. Closed for the duration it might be, but a skeleton staff would still be in residence, if only to keep the fires going and the rooms clean.

I arrived on Mrs. Hennessey's doorstep, tired, unhappy, and uncertain about my future.

Accustomed to our coming and going at all hours, she welcomed me warmly, clearly curious to know where I had been and if I'd sorted out my problem with the Nursing Service.

I had not. It would be useless to try. But I told her that a friend in Paris had died, and I had had no time to think about myself.

"I'm so sorry, my dear," she said, over the cup of tea she had made for me, late as it was. "I didn't know. Was that the letter from France that you'd been expecting?"

"Yes. It was waiting for me in Aldshot. Thank you for forwarding it."

"I wondered that it might be bad news," she said, nodding, "coming all the way from France." It sounded as if France was as far away as China, and I smiled.

"That's better," she applauded. "You have such a lovely smile, my dear."

"Is there any other mail for me?"

There was, a letter from Cousin Bruce and a parcel with no return address.

"Go on, open them," she urged. "I don't mind, I'll just take the tea things through to the kitchen."

Left alone in Mrs. Hennessey's small dining room I opened the parcel first, thinking it might have been forwarded from Cornwall.

Inside was a folded copy of the *Times*. As I drew it out, a slip of paper fluttered to the carpet, landing at my feet. I retrieved it and read the message.

We kept your name out of it, but we have in custody a ring of thieves, our receiver of stolen goods, and our murderer—the man you identified. We are very grateful.

It was signed by Inspector Morgan. I unfolded the newspaper and saw the headlines in bold black letters.

SCOTLAND YARD: ARREST OF MURDERER AND

BAND OF RUTHLESS THIEVES

That was good news. I was glad I'd taken the time to go to the Yard.

Setting the newspaper aside to read later, I turned to Bruce's letter.

It had been written two weeks before. Bruce was much improved and had been given leave to travel to Scotland. He had graduated to two canes and hoped to need only one before very long. He had wanted to see me, if I was in London when he came through to make his connection. But he expected I would be back in France by that time.

I reread the last part, frowning over it. Bruce knew, I had told him myself, that I had been forced to resign from the Nursing Service. He couldn't have known about the letter from Madeleine that had taken me back to Paris. And yet he wrote as if he thought I was still a Sister, serving in France once more, for he ended the letter with, *Be safe, my dear girl.*

Mrs. Hennessey came back into the room and spotted the newspaper. "Oh, the *Times*. Did someone send you a copy? It was all very exciting, I can tell you. Looting from those poor Belgians and the French, theft of precious objects, murder. Quite the most amazing events." Looking up, she saw my face. "Are you all right, Elspeth, dear? Your letter wasn't more bad news, was it?" she asked, concerned for me.

"I'm a little confused," I said. "My cousin thinks I'm back in France. But I told him myself that I'd had to resign because his father disapproved."

"Is he delirious, dear? Has he taken a turn for the worse?"

"No, no, he's convalescent, he was on the point of leaving for Scotland, to visit his father. He must have been considered well enough to make the journey."

"Well," she said thoughtfully, "there's that other letter that came for you. From the Nursing Service. The same day I saw you and told you about the letter from France. I'd just sent it along to Aldshot. Did you find it?"

But it hadn't come. Only the letter from Madeleine had reached me there. And I had been in a mad rush to get back to London after reading her news. I hadn't waited for it to arrive.

"Surely it was sent back to you here," I suggested. "Since I wasn't there, they would have guessed where to find me."

She smiled. "Yes, but perhaps they expected you to return? Did you tell them you'd be away for some time?"

Peter would have waited for me. He must have stayed on for several more weeks. Weeks wondering where I was, wondering why I hadn't written. I twisted the ruby ring on my finger.

Surely Peter wasn't still in Aldshot? Surely he'd have sent the letter back to Mrs. Hennessey and the flat, before he left. Then where was the letter? Had he simply set it on the mantel shelf in the cottage, next to my Christmas ring, thinking that one day, someday, I would come back? Or had he been too angry with me to care? It wasn't the first time I'd left him without a word. I couldn't blame him.

I sat there, thinking hard.

I must find that letter. If I couldn't go back to Peter, at least I'd have my nursing. Something salvaged out of the wreckage of my life. Was I strong enough to go to Aldshot, and if Peter was still there, tell him the truth about Alain? I didn't know. I owed it to him to try.

I needed a motorcar to reach the village. Where on earth was I to find one?

I said, "Do you know anyone who has a motorcar, Mrs. Hennessey? I want to borrow one."

"A motorcar, my dear? I can't think of anyone. Bess has one, I believe, but it's stored in Somerset."

"Too far. Let me think." I went through a mental list of my acquaintances who lived in London and who owned a motorcar. It wasn't a very long list, but the name that leapt out at me was Timothy Howard's.

I rose, already planning what I must say to him. And then I remembered how late it was.

Tomorrow. I'd have to wait until tomorrow.

Thwarted. I had to laugh at my impatience. The letter had waited all this time, it could wait another day.

"It's been a tiring journey. I should go up to bed. Is anyone else here?"

"That's a very good idea, my dear. Things always look better in the morning, don't they? And you'll have the flat to yourself. Bess left two days ago, Diana has leave and is visiting her family, and Mary is still in France."

I thanked her, climbed the long flight of stairs, and once in the flat with the door shut on the world, I simply went to bed. There was nothing more I could do.

The next morning, I went in search of Timothy, and I finally ran him to earth just before the noon hour. He had gone to his club for lunch and a meeting there, and so I had to ask the staff if they would tell him I was waiting. I was allowed to stand in the foyer, for it was overcast and spitting something that might be rain or sleet.

Two minutes later, he came running down the stairs and greeted me warmly. His uniform was freshly pressed, creases sharp as knives. He was attached to the War Office. But I was reminded of Henri's arrival at the Villard house, his uniform stained and wrinkled.

"Lady Elspeth, it's wonderful to see you. How are you? More to the point, how is Bruce?"

"He's in Scotland. They gave him leave to go home to finish his convalescence."

"Oh, that *is* good news."

"Timothy, I've come to ask a favor. An important letter has gone astray. I think it's in Sussex, and I need to go there straightaway to retrieve it. The nearest railway station is miles away and there's weather coming in. Is your motorcar still in London? Could I possibly borrow it for a day?"

He frowned. "That's a long drive alone. Are you sure you can manage?"

I wanted to tell him I'd already driven that journey several times over, but I said cheerfully, "Yes, of course, I wouldn't ask if I felt it was too much."

"It's in the mews behind my flat. Number sixteen. Tell them it's all right if you borrow it. But if you have any doubts, someone there should be able to go with you."

That was the last thing I wanted. But I thanked him for his suggestion.

"You owe me a chance to take you out to dinner one night," he said, smiling. "I don't think we've had dinner together since before the war started."

"Done," I said, and turned to leave, eager to be on my way. I was halfway out the door when he called to me.

"Lady Elspeth, I'd almost forgot. There's news of Peter—"

"Yes, I've heard," I said, waving a hand in acknowledgment. But the truth was, I didn't want news of Peter. Not now. *I mustn't think about Peter . . .*

"Good," he said, and was away up the stairs to his meeting.

I found the mews and number sixteen. A man came running to pull open the doors, and there was Timothy's motorcar. I told the man that I was borrowing it for two days, and he too looked askance. I assured him that I was perfectly capable, but he watched me bring the motorcar out and drive it down the lane to the street.

It was still spitting a cold rain when I reached the main road out of London and turned toward Portsmouth. But that was crowded with convoys, and I soon struck inland, toward Midhurst, and from there south.

I heard the clock in the village just before Aldshot striking the hour as I passed through, and I counted to nine. My headlamps barely pierced what seemed to be sleet on the verge of snow. My windscreen wipers kept up, but I had to peer out at the road to see where I was going. I could feel my shoulders, stiff with cold and tension, knotting as I leaned forward.

Aldshot's church tower loomed ahead on my left, and just beyond I could pick out the cottage. It was dark—I'd expected that. Even at this distance I had the feeling that it was empty. Closed. No motorcar out front. Just as well, I told myself. There was lamplight in the Wright house, and so I pulled up by the path to their door, and got out. My knees ached from sitting so long in the cold motorcar, for the heater did little more than warm my feet.

Walking briskly up to the door, I knocked and then waited. A curtain in the front-room window twitched.

After a moment or two, Mrs. Wright opened the door and exclaimed in surprise. "I saw the motorcar, my dear, and I thought, surely someone's lost his way in this weather. I never dreamed—is there anyone else with you?" She was peering around my shoulder to see.

"I'm quite alone. It's a borrowed motorcar, and I must have it back by tomorrow."

"Come in," she said, realizing she was keeping me standing on her doorstep. "The kettle is already on, and Joel will be back soon, I hope. He had to take old Harry Clinton into Midhurst. His sciatica is bothering him again. Have you had your dinner? There's food in the pantry—"

She was running on, words tumbling over themselves.

I followed her into the sitting room where I had taken my breakfast all those weeks before. I felt a tug at my heart as the memories came rushing back. She had been clearing away the table, and there was only a teacup and a dish of parsnips still there, as if I'd interrupted her on her way to the kitchen.

She offered me a chair by the hearth, and then finished clearing away, whisking out a clean white tablecloth for my supper.

"Please don't go to any trouble—"

"It's no trouble at all. And you'll stay the night, won't you? There's weather coming in and you shouldn't be on the road all alone."

I thanked her for her kindness, and then, as the stream of words seemed to slow at last, I managed to say, "You have another letter that's waiting for me, I think."

She stared at me.

"From London. From Queen Alexandra's—"

"Of course! It's in the desk there, let me fetch it for you."

She hurried across to the little desk by the window, let down the top, and reached into a pigeonhole for an envelope.

"I didn't know when you might be coming back. Or where to send it. I asked the Captain what I should do, and he told me to hold on to it. That he believed you'd come back to us. And he was right, you have."

I couldn't bear to hear about Peter.

Turning away, I opened the letter from QAIMNS.

It wasn't an official notification of my resignation.

On the contrary, it informed me that there had been a mistake made, and that I was reinstated without prejudice. I was to report to the London headquarters as soon as practical to resume my duties as a Sister.

I couldn't believe the evidence of my own eyes. I read it again, and then a third time.

What had happened? Surely Cousin Kenneth hadn't relented and changed his mind.

It was very unlike him, once a decision had been taken.

Bruce—

I had told Bruce what had happened, and how upset I was over his father's high-handedness in forcing me to resign.

Dear Bruce, had he intervened on my behalf, had he told his father to change his opinion of what Queen Alexandra's Imperial Military Nursing Service had done for wounded and dying men?

Cousin Kenneth was from another generation. Perhaps he had been made to see that times had changed, and that women of my class had not put themselves beyond the pale by doing their duty for King and Country. After all, Queen Alexandra, widow of the late King Edward, was the royal patroness. She wouldn't have agreed to allow her name to be used if she had had any reservations about the Service.

Whatever had happened, I felt as if my life had been turned round, that after so much unhappiness, I could at least return to the work I did so well.

I smiled, looked up at Mrs. Wright, and said, "It's good news. I'm so glad I came down."

"Yes, dear, that's wonderful. We could all use good news from time to time."

She brought me in a cup of tea, some fresh bread, slices of cold chicken, a dish of parsnips and carrots roasted in her oven, and a pudding.

"It's not much," she apologized, "but it will keep starvation from your door."

I thanked her for her generosity and ate with more appetite than I had felt in weeks.

I had finished the pudding, and she was removing the dishes, when I realized that there was something on her mind. Was she wondering where I had been? Why I never came back to Peter or Aldshot?

I owed her an explanation, but all I could say was, "A dear friend was very ill in Paris. I had to go. I had to be there with the family."

"I'm sorry to hear it, my dear. Has she recovered?"

"It was her brother who was recovering from severe wounds. He—he died."

"How sad. Let's hope he's in a better place now. I've come to believe that, seeing the wounded as I do from time to time. For some there's no hope of a good tomorrow."

It was well put, and I nodded.

"Is that his ring?" she asked, curiosity overcoming good manners.

"It was a family heirloom," I answered. "I've known him for many years, and he asked me to wear it in remembrance."

"The war has taken away so many good men," she said in sympathy, then urged me to move closer to the fire. After fussing with the grate, she straightened and said diffidently, "There's another letter for you. Well, not really a letter. I wasn't sure whether I should mention it, as you didn't ask."

"A letter? From whom?" Please God, not from Peter. I couldn't bear it.

She went back to the desk and drew out another envelope. I saw at once that there was no stamp on it. And I knew then that Peter had left it for me. And I had treated him so shabbily.

I opened it slowly, turning a little so that Mrs. Wright couldn't see my face. But she busied herself with the dishes, giving me a measure of privacy. I was reminded of Mrs. Hennessey, doing the very same thing.

It was a short letter.

Where are you? I wish I knew. It's been the very devil, wondering. I'm well enough now to leave the cottage and return to my flat. Mrs. Wright said you'd come back for a letter from France. I'd always thought there might be someone else, possibly in Paris. There was that other ring, you see. And you never told me you loved me. I wish him well. I don't know what to do about my ring now. I was going to leave it on the mantel shelf, but that wouldn't do, if someone else came here before you returned. Or perhaps you'll never return. And so I took it out and buried it at the foot of the walnut tree. It belongs here. And here it will stay. I love you enough to wish you happiness, wherever you are. God keep you safe.

And it was signed simply, *Peter.*

I sat down in a chair by the table. I wanted to cry, for Peter, for myself. For Alain.

After a moment I said to Mrs. Wright, fighting to keep my voice steady, "Do you have a trowel? Could I borrow it, please?"

She stared at me. "There's one out in the shed, of course. Joel's. Why should you need a trowel, my dear? In this weather?"

"It's important. It's something Peter—Captain Gilchrist left for me. Please?"

For a moment she hesitated, for it must have seemed to her a mad request, and then with a nod she left the room. After a few minutes she was back again, an old and well-used trowel in her hand. "It's snowing, surely it can wait until tomorrow? Whatever it is?"

"It can't wait. It's waited too long already. Bless you."

Taking the trowel, I put on my coat and hat, wrapped my scarf around my throat, and went out the door. I knew Mrs. Wright was anxiously watching from the window. *I'll explain later,* I thought. *Once I have it safe. Then she'll understand.*

It was already a little slippery underfoot, and great white flakes were falling silently from the sky, softly touching my face, sticking to my coat. If this continues, I thought, by tomorrow I shan't know where to dig.

I crossed the road, went through the hedge, and knelt at the foot of the walnut tree, feeling with my fingers for any sign of loose earth. And there it was, just in front of me.

I began to dig very carefully, scraping at the earth until I heard the trowel's edge strike something that must be metal.

It took me another five minutes to winkle it out of the cold ground. Then I saw what it was. A Princess Mary Christmas Box, the small metal tin that was given to every member of the Army and Navy, containing a gift of chocolate and tobacco and other necessities, from a grateful nation. Acceptance of the truth, that the war wouldn't—couldn't—be over by Christmas.

Still kneeling on the snow-wet ground, I opened it. In the distance I could hear the jingle of harness and the hoof-beats of horses as a carriage came down the road. Ignoring it, I opened the box and looked inside.

A small square of silk lay there, and on it the ring that Peter had made for me. A simple thing, carved from a pig bone.

I closed my fingers over it, my eyes shut, remembering when the bare tree above my head was lit with the light of dozens of candles, flickering in the dark.

The carriage turned into the farmyard just past the Wrights' house, and I knew Joel must have made it home safely from Midhurst. But I ignored him, trying to hold fast to that memory, trying to hear Peter's voice again, and feel the warmth of his shoulder touching mine as we stood close together by the window, looking out at the Christmas gift of the village to two strangers in their midst.

But it was slipping away, in spite of all I could do.

I felt hot tears running down my face. "Please come back," I whispered to the fading image in my mind. "Just this once, please let me remember."

Joel's voice, clear in the quiet of the snowfall, was calling to his wife as he unhitched the horses and took them into the barn. And my memory seemed to shatter with the distraction.

The ring in my palm was cold from being in the ground. I couldn't warm it.

"Elspeth?"

I knelt there, unable to move.

And then I felt his hands on my shoulders, pulling me to my feet. My hat went flying.

"I don't know where you've been," Peter said softly, his lips against my hair. "Or why. It doesn't matter. Nothing matters but the fact that I've found you again."

I turned in his arms, and he held me tight, as if afraid I might vanish into the night.

"Your wound," I said, anxious not to hurt him.

He laughed, that deep chuckle rumbling in his chest. "In another month, six weeks at the most, I'll be rejoining my regiment."

"But what are you doing here? Mrs. Wright—"

"I was on my way here. I ran into Howard in London. He'd just seen you, he said you'd borrowed his motorcar, something about a letter in Sussex. I drove like a madman until I had a flat tire on the road outside Midhurst. Joel was coming back from taking one of the farmers in to see the doctor. He found me, brought me the rest of the way. I was afraid I'd missed you, that you'd turned back to London in this weather."

Before I could say anything, in the soft light from the snow falling over us he saw the ring on my finger, dull gold and ruby red. He pulled away.

"He was Madeleine's brother. Alain," I said quickly. "He lost his arm fighting on the Marne, and he couldn't bear that. He killed himself. If he'd lived, I'd have married him, Peter. He asked me, long before I met you again and fell in love with you. And I would have kept faith with him because he needed me. I wear his ring still because he was a brave and honorable man, and I was very fond of him. But *this* is the ring that I will keep until I am old, because you gave it to me." I held it out in my palm, for him to see.

He took it from me and put it on my finger.

"I'll give you another. As soon as I've gone to Scotland. And you'll travel with me. I'm damned if I'm going to risk losing you again."

I was supposed to report to the Nursing Service for duty as soon as practicable.

But QAIMNS had waited this long. They could wait another few weeks. Peter kissed me then, standing under the bare branches of the walnut tree.